DARKNESS THREATENING

Dirk Greyson

Published by

DREAMSPINNER PRESS

5032 Capital Circle SW, Suite 2, PMB# 279, Tallahassee, FL 32305-7886 USA
www.dreamspinnerpress.com

Darkness Threatening
© 2016 Dirk Greyson.

Cover Art
© 2016 Reese Dante.
http://www.reesedante.com
Cover content is for illustrative purposes only and any person depicted on the cover is a model.

ISBN: 978-1-63476-916-7
Digital ISBN: 978-1-63476-917-4
Library of Congress Control Number: 2015918975
Published February 2016
v. 1.0

Printed in the United States of America
∞

This paper meets the requirements of
ANSI/NISO Z39.48-1992 (Permanence of Paper).

Readers love *Challenge the Darkness* by DIRK GREYSON

"*Challenge the Darkness* by Dirk Greyson is another fine story to add to the paranormal genre. With passion, action and realistic characters, this story is a must read for fans of this genre."
　　　　　　—Joyfully Jay

"I adored this story."
　　　　　　—Prism Book Alliance

"The plot as a whole kept me interested throughout the entire book and none of it felt overdone. I would very much like to see some more books come out of this 'world.'"
　　　　　　—Two Chicks Obsessed with Books and Eye Candy

"Dirk Greyson writes a hell of a story, no matter what name or genre he chooses."
　　　　　　—The Novel Approach

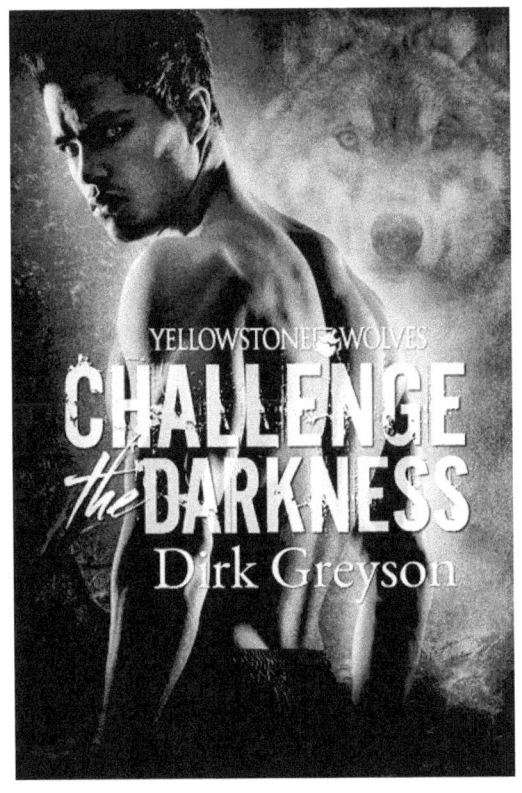

"…a really good book and I would definitely recommend this!"
　　　　　　—Inked Rainbow Reviews

"…if you're looking for an action-packed read full of tension, passion, and two mates clearly meant to be together, then you will probably like this novel. I certainly hope there are more stories set in this world!"
　　　　　　—Rainbow Book Reviews

By DIRK GREYSON

An Assassin's Holiday

DAY AND KNIGHT
Day and Knight
Sun and Shadow

YELLOWSTONE WOLVES
Challenge the Darkness
Darkness Threatening

Published by DREAMSPINNER PRESS
www.dreamspinnerpress.com

This entire series is because of Kate Douglas's incredible work.
You are amazing!!!

CHAPTER 1

"I DON'T give a shit about what they taught you at that ridiculous school," Juneau yelled as he stood from the table and stalked over to Fredrik, who was determined not to show fear in any way. Juneau might be his brother, but there was absolutely no love lost between them. "I don't know where you learned that being a fucking fairy who takes it up the ass was all right, but in this pack, it certainly is not." Juneau backhanded Fredrik across the cheek, sending him reeling in a circle.

Fredrik caught the table to keep from going down to the floor. "Screw you, Juneau. You're the one who doesn't know shit about anything. I am who I am, and there isn't a damn thing you can do about it. Dad is dead and you're living in this shithole cabin on the edge of nowhere." He stood back up.

"Are you challenging me?" Juneau growled. "Because I'll gut you like a rabbit if you ever talk to me like that again." He stepped closer once again.

"Yeah, I know. You're the alpha... of nothing."

"I'm your alpha and don't you forget it. I may be living in this piece of shit, but I won't be for long."

"Where is everyone else?" Fredrik meant it dismissively, but the stare he got was cold enough to freeze water on the equator.

"They're coming. Those loyal to Father were scattered after his downfall last summer, but I've put out word to those who were most loyal. They'll all be here in three days, and then I'll start building my own pack, taking back what should have been mine in the first place. And you, dear brother, will stand at my side, keep your smart mouth shut, and do what I say. There will be no weakness in this pack, and

1

that means no males taking it up the ass. You will mate and have litters of pups. We need our numbers to grow as quickly as possible."

"Why would I want to go along with what you want?" Fredrik was surprised at himself and wondered where he found the courage to speak up. He'd always been the quiet one. Their father, Anton, hadn't been interested in anything that didn't involve fighting, brute strength, and power. Those three things were all that had counted, what he'd lived for, as essential to him and his wolf as oxygen.

"Because I'm your alpha and a hell of a lot stronger than you. And because I'll kill you slowly and painfully if you don't." Juneau stood and glanced at the nearest chair, then back at him. He glared at Fredrik with the intensity of one of the lasers he'd seen at school. "I'm waiting."

Fredrik picked up the chair and brought it to his brother, who sat as though he were a king. But there was no kingdom. When their father lost his challenge to Mikael Volokov, the alpha of the Old Faithful pack, everything changed. They were outcasts—all of their father's family was—tainted with his dark madness and obsession with power. Fredrik had been the only one to escape much of the fallout because Anton had sent him to college. He'd said he wanted Fredrik to learn the ways of men and the outside world, probably so he could extend his power there as well. Thankfully, his father had provided enough money for him to almost finish school. There wasn't quite enough, though, and that had given Juneau power. If Fredrik wanted to graduate, then he had to submit. This discussion was the culmination of that decision—one Fredrik now realized could be the biggest mistake of his life.

Fredrik had thought he was out of the family and had gotten away from them. This was not the life he wanted, and his father's death had raised the possibility of him just fading away. He'd hoped he could find a new pack and start a whole new life. Now that wasn't to be. Tuition increases had left him with little choice but to approach his brother, and now he was stuck.

"You'll live in this house, where I can keep an eye on you. The room you've been using will be your home." Juneau looked up, and

2

the woman who had been working at the stove, doing her best to look the other way and pretend she saw and heard nothing, rushed over and placed a plate in front of Juneau. He didn't acknowledge her in any way other than with a glance before he began to eat.

Fredrik stifled a cringe. He'd been sleeping in that room for two nights. Well, there had been very little sleeping, given the fact that his brother spent much of the past two nights making as much carnal noise as possible. Juneau was insatiable and had sex with as many as three females a night. Like their father, he felt it was his duty to father as many pups as he could. He was the alpha male, and, as such, he had the pick of anyone he wanted.

"Hearing how a man behaves will be good for you," Juneau continued, pulling Fredrik out of his thoughts. "You will also ask permission before you leave the compound, and you will talk to no one unless I expressly permit it. Somehow I will make a real man out of…." He waved his hand in Fredrik's direction. "This." He shook his head. "How you ever came from our father is beyond me."

The door opened and Yuri, his brother's beta and partner in crime and punishment since they were children, strode into the room and sat.

"Inge," Juneau said. It was the first time his brother had used the woman's name since Fredrik had been there. At least Fredrik knew what it was now.

She made up another plate and set it in front of Yuri. Fredrik was starving, but he made no move to sit. The idea of sharing a meal of any kind with his brother was about as appetizing as eating mud between two pieces of crap.

"Dimitri called, and he has a surprise for you," Yuri said gleefully, his eyes filled with evil mirth.

Fredrik went cold, wondering what Yuri and his twin brother were up to. Yuri and Dimitri were two peas in a pod and thought alike. Truthfully, it was more likely that they shared a single brain between them. Neither was at all bright, but they were ruthless and believed in taking what they wanted.

"He'll be here in an hour."

"What kind of surprise?" Juneau snapped and blew a breath out his nose. "Sit down!" he demanded, and Fredrik did as he was told.

Inge brought a plate for him. He smiled at her and thanked her softly. Inge actually looked as though she wasn't quite sure how to process the simple politeness. She eventually nodded and scampered away like a scared deer.

"He said that it was an accessory for your bedroom and that you were going to love it."

Fredrik managed to keep from cringing. God knew what his brother's demented cronies had come up with now, but it couldn't be good. He ate, but the food tasted like nothing at all. Fredrik was eating only to eat. Tasting what was in his mouth was nearly impossible. He was a prisoner here; that was all there was to it. He needed to figure out a way to get out of here, and he needed to do it fast.

When he was done, Fredrik took his plate to the sink and made to go to his room. He needed to get away.

"Sit back down," Juneau said, and Fredrik sighed and sat once again. "Our time is coming very soon. I can feel it. The packs that splintered once Father died are still trying to get on their feet. Volokov is stretched way too thin, and while all those new alphas may have voted him as high alpha or whatever they're calling it, he can't be everywhere." Juneau grinned.

"What are we going to do?" Yuri asked, rubbing his hands together. "I want to get my hands on him alone, just for a few minutes."

Juneau jumped to his feet, his chair tumbling backward to the floor. "Volokov is mine, pure and simple." He gripped the edge of the table and leaned closer to Yuri. "You got that?"

"Yeah, of course," Yuri said, baring his neck slightly.

"Good. He killed my father, and I'm going to get back everything my father had and more, because I'm going to get Old Faithful too. All of it."

Yuri showed some intelligence—or maybe it was simple self-preservation—and nodded, and Juneau slowly sat back down.

Fredrik wanted to ask how his brother thought he was going to bring that about. The other packs had united under Volokov, and they were stronger now that they had one person they all trusted. But Fredrik said nothing because he didn't feel like getting hit again.

He ended up sitting at the table for another hour listening to Yuri and Juneau talk over all their grandiose plans that meant absolutely nothing. Juneau was as ruthless as their father, but he was also crazier, if that was possible.

A truck pulled up outside; the deep rumble told him it was big, probably to compensate for something. When the clatter stopped, a door squeaked open and closed, followed by another. Then Dimitri slithered in like the snake version of a wolf that he was. Where Yuri was strong and tended to stomp, Dimitri was sneaky and stalked around behind things.

"I got you a present," he said to Juneau. "You want me to deliver it?" He smiled, showing off his missing front tooth. It made him look more like a yokel than his brother, but looks were deceiving.

"Sure." Juneau sat back and waited while Dimitri went back out to his truck.

Fredrik was ashamed, but he turned to watch as well. He swallowed hard and nearly vomited his lunch when he saw Dimitri come in carrying someone over his shoulder. It was a girl, probably about sixteen, and she was a pretty young thing. Definitely a wolf, and a strong one.

Juneau grinned, and Fredrik wrinkled his nose when he smelled his brother's arousal. "She's a kid."

"Mind your own business. She's old enough to have pups, and by God I think she'll have one of mine."

She began to struggle and whimper. There was fight in her, which Fredrik was happy about, though it wasn't likely to do her any good. Lord knew his brother had no compunction about taking whatever he wanted.

"Put her in my room. I think I'll savor this one for a little while."

Dimitri carried the girl, who was tied hand and foot, across the room and dumped her on the sofa. Her eyes were wild, and she bit at the gag in her mouth. The scent of fear filled the room, but it was tempered with bravery and strength. Fredrik knew she would need both of those to survive.

"You rape children now," Fredrik said as he got up and went toward the room he'd been assigned.

"There's no rape about it. She wants me, I can see it in her eyes, and by tonight, this little thing is going to scream for me. Aren't you?" Juneau patted her cheek, and Fredrik went ice cold.

Dimitri lifted the girl off the sofa and carried her toward the bedroom, where she would likely be kept tied up until Juneau was ready for her.

The thought that he was going to have to hear his brother.... Jesus.... Fredrik hurried to the bathroom and closed the door. His lunch made a second appearance, and he flushed it down as quickly as possible. If his brother heard or smelled what was happening, there would be hell to pay all over again.

He closed the toilet lid and sat. He could barely hear them through the door, but at times their voices boomed as they laughed and joked about the fun Juneau was going to have when he deflowered the girl waiting in the bedroom. Jesus, they were sick, and if his stomach weren't already empty, it would be again. What was wrong with his brother?

Okay, half brother. Thank goodness they didn't have the same mother. Maybe that was the difference. He and Juneau certainly had the same father; there was no denying that. The near-black eyes were a giveaway. Most of Anton's children had them, and Juneau had plenty of half brothers and half sisters. Their father had been as sexually driven as Juneau was. The family had scattered after their father's demise, and now it looked like Juneau was trying to pull everyone together again. Jesus....

Fredrik flushed the toilet again and opened the bathroom door. He heard the three of them still talking, much softer now, but that didn't matter. He could still hear them. Juneau had a good sense of smell, but his hearing wasn't as keen as Fredrik's, a fact Fredrik kept to himself. In Anton's family, pack members learned to capitalize on any advantage to survive, and more than once Fredrik had heard anger flow from his father or brothers and conveniently managed to get out of their way until they'd had a chance to cool off.

"Let's go for a run. I need to hunt something," Juneau said as Fredrik reached the door to his room and went inside. He closed the door as silently as he could and stood stock-still, trying not to breathe so he could hear them.

The front door opened and closed. Fredrik hoped they had all gone, but it was likely one of the dipshit twins had been left behind. He listened at the door and then opened it slightly, scenting for anyone in the house. He could smell fear and hear soft sobs from the room next door, but that was all. He stepped out of the room as a chair scraped on the floor. Just as he suspected. Squaring his shoulders, Fredrik walked back toward the open central room.

Dimitri sat at the table, staring off into space. "What are you up to? Juneau said I was to stay here and keep an eye on you and his present." He grinned like an idiot. "But I was thinking that maybe you could be my present." He stood. "A hole's a hole, right? Besides, I bet you'd like what I got for you."

Fredrik swallowed hard. "I don't think so. You aren't my type."

"I ain't, huh? I'm a guy and you like guys, so I figured I could see what all the fuss was about." He stepped closer, and Fredrik took a small step back. Dimitri stomped his foot and then laughed. "I ain't gonna soil myself with the likes of you. You can stop looking like you're gonna jump through the roof." He walked to the small table near the old sofa, yanked open the drawer, and pulled out a deck of cards. He began shuffling again and again, the snap and thump sounds filling the small space.

Fredrik's throat was bone dry, so he pulled open the refrigerator door and got some water. Inge had left too, so it was only Dimitri and him. His gaze kept going to the door of Juneau's room. There was a girl in there frightened half to death. The scent was enough to turn his stomach again. He opened the bottle, rinsed his mouth, and spat into the sink. Then he took a long drink, the liquid settling in his stomach with a hollow thud. He closed the door and opened one of the kitchen drawers. He needed a weapon, anything at hand, if he was to have a chance against Dimitri. The guy was smaller than Yuri, but Fredrik was no match for him physically. Hell, he wasn't a physical match for anyone in his family. His father had always called him his runt pup.

"What are you up to?" Dimitri didn't even look up from his game.

"Just getting some water. You want some?"

"Nah. Get me a beer, though," he said and played another card. "I got eyes in the back of my head. I'll know if you pull anything."

Fredrik opened the refrigerator again and got a beer. As he closed the door and pulled open the drawer next to it, he had to keep himself from whooping for joy. He'd found the knives. He picked out one and then carried the beer over to Dimitri and set it on the table.

"I know what you're doing," Dimitri said and grabbed his hand. "I know everything, and you're just some runt. So don't be thinking you're going to try anything so you can get away. If I let you leave, Juneau will have my nuts, and I want them right where they are. And the only way you're getting out of here is if I let you leave."

"Is that so?" Fredrik jerked away and plunged the knife into Dimitri's neck before pushing him forward onto the table. He managed to get out of the way of the blood, but it sprayed all over the floor. "You may think I'm small, you piece of shit, but I've got fight in me," he said to blank eyes as Dimitri went completely still.

Fredrik's heart beat a mile a minute as he backed away, trying not to slip on the growing slick of blood, and headed right for Juneau's room. He pulled open the door and gasped. The girl lay on the bed, tied at her ankles and wrists. She was covered by a sheet, but it was clear she was otherwise naked. Her amber eyes were big as saucers, and if he swung that way, he'd say she was one of the prettiest young women he'd ever seen.

"I'm not going to hurt you, but we need to get out of here." Fredrik untied her wrists and removed the gag. "You have to be quiet. Get the ropes off your feet, and I'll bring you something to wear." Fredrik was already on the move. He avoided Dimitri when he left the room and went to his own. He grabbed a shirt and sweatpants from his drawer, along with a pair of heavy socks. He didn't have shoes for her, but this would have to do. When Fredrik got back, the girl was on her feet with the sheet clutched around her. "We have to be out of here in two minutes," he said.

She nodded and took the clothes.

Fredrik went back to his room for the last time and grabbed the few things that were important: his phone, his wallet, and a picture of his mother. He also took his secret stash of money. When he came out of the room, the girl was dressed, standing in the doorway. He took her hand as he went by and practically dragged her toward the front door of the cabin.

"Shit," Fredrik swore.

"What?"

"I need keys." He returned to Dimitri and fished around in his pockets. He came up with his phone and then his keys. Fredrik also grabbed his wallet, took the cash, and then dropped everything else on the floor. "Got 'em."

He led the girl outside and over to Dimitri's truck. It was the only new thing in the entire area. Fredrik opened the door and climbed in. He waited for the girl, then started the engine and pulled out as fast as he dared once the doors were closed. "What pack are you?" Fredrik asked.

"Why?" she asked, pressed to the door, as far away from him as possible.

"So I can get you home."

"My uncle is the alpha of the Old Faithful Pack," she answered.

Jesus Christ. Fredrik wondered if Yuri and Dimitri had known who she was. Not that it seemed to matter to them. They were all about taking whatever or whomever they wanted.

"Okay. I can get you to that area, and then you'll need to direct me to your pack compound."

"You're really going to take me home?" He could hear the disbelief just a fraction of an inch from the surface.

"Yes. Of course I am. But first I have to get as far away from here as possible."

"Did you really kill that other wolf? You're not much bigger than I am."

"I used a knife, but yeah. I stabbed him in the throat. I couldn't let them hurt you." His hand shook and the truck briefly went up on two wheels when he took a turn a little too fast, but he needed speed and distance. If they were caught, he'd end up as dead as Dimitri, and the girl would suffer a fate worse than she would have before he'd tried to rescue her.

"Why?" she whispered. "You have the same eyes as the guy in charge."

"He's my asshole half brother. I'm Fredrik Romanov and I won't hurt you. So there's no need to plaster yourself to the door."

She relaxed slightly. "Jane," she said with surprising strength. "Jane Stephenson."

He raised his eyebrows at the last name. It wasn't what he would have expected.

"My mother is Alpha Volokov's sister." She held on as he picked up speed and made the turn onto the main road through the park.

Soon they were joined by other traffic, and Fredrik felt somewhat better, even though he was driving the truck of a dead guy. Well, that guy was a wolf, and there was no way Juneau would ever call the police. The last thing he wanted was them nosing around his business. Juneau would be angry enough to rip the cabin apart with his bare hands, but he certainly wasn't going to call anyone for help. He'd exact his revenge on Fredrik personally and with as much brutality as possible. Fredrik had no doubt about that whatsoever.

"It's good to meet you. I sincerely wish it had been under better circumstances." Fredrik dug into his pocket and pulled out his phone. He unlocked it and handed it to Jane. "Call your family. Tell them that you're safe and that you're on your way home."

Jane nodded and began punching the numbers. Fredrik knew as soon as someone answered because Jane broke down in tears. "I'm okay, Mama. Fredrik rescued me, and he's bringing me home." She composed herself quickly and the tears stopped. "No one hurt me, but they would have. I was only frightened." Dang, Jane had a lot more guts and internal strength than Fredrik had given her credit for.

"Tell her we're coming through the park as quickly as we can in a dark gray Chevy truck. We should be nearing your pack territory in an hour." Traffic thinned out a little, and Fredrik drove as fast as he dared. Every mile put him farther from his brother and brought Jane closer to safety.

Jane relayed the message. "Tell Uncle Mikael that I'm okay." There was a short pause. "It's me, Uncle Mikael. ... Yes, I'm really okay. ... I went into town, remember? I was doing some of the shopping for Gran. ... Yes, I'm okay. It was frightening, but no one hurt me, although Fredrik killed someone to rescue me. And he drives like Uncle Karl." There was a hint of mirth in her voice. "I love you too. I'll call when we get close to pack land." She hung up and held on to the phone. After a few seconds, the phone rang and Jane answered it. "Daddy, I'm okay." Now she started to cry. "I really am. Fredrik saved me, and he—they'll kill him if they find him." She listened for a few minutes, then said good-bye and hung up.

"Let's just get you home," Fredrik said. Then he'd figure out how to get as far away from his brother as humanly possible. Maybe he'd get a different car and head all the way east. He might be able to find a pack there he could join. Maybe there was a pack in the country who hadn't heard of his father.

Jane grew quiet, and Fredrik sank into his own thoughts.

"You'll want to turn off about five miles ahead," Jane said as they drove deeper into the park. "The road is paved for a few miles, and then it turns to gravel. That's the pack boundary, and I expect my family will meet us there."

"All right," Fredrik said.

She went back to riding in silence for a few minutes, and Fredrik let the truck chew up the miles. "Why did you do it?" Jane asked. "You risked a lot to save me, and you killed the man who took me."

"He deserved it. No one should be forced to do what my brother was planning. He was going to take what wasn't his and what you were never prepared to give him."

"I heard what that guy said to you."

"Yeah, well, people like me aren't welcome in my brother's pack."

"Not everyone is like that." Jane seemed to have some of her earlier confidence back. "No one would dare say anything like that in Old Faithful. Uncle Mikael and Uncle Denton wouldn't allow it. They believe that everyone deserves a safe place to be themselves."

"I take it you've heard the speech before," Fredrik said, and Jane nodded and smiled.

The sun was setting behind them when Fredrik reached the Old Faithful boundary. He pulled to a stop when half a dozen vehicles blocked his way. A crowd of people waited by the side of the road, and they all clustered around Jane when she got out of the truck.

Fredrik opened his door and stood behind it, letting everyone welcome Jane home. It was a warm scene, the likes of which Fredrik had seen very few times in his life. Warmth and tenderness were not part of his father's way of doing anything, and a stab of jealousy went through him as he realized just what he'd been missing all his life.

Voices overlapped one another, except these were happy and joyful. That was another sound that was nearly foreign to him. Laughter, cheering, happiness—not part of his life. Mostly Fredrik tried to hide and stay out of everyone's way. His mother had been the only person who had ever showed him any affection at all, and that had ended at sixteen. So yeah, fuck it all, he was jealous as hell of Jane. An entire group of wolves was happy to have her back. He stayed away, not wanting to intrude on their happiness and not quite understanding how to deal with it.

"Uncle Mikael, this is Fredrik," Jane said, and the largest wolf he'd ever seen walked over to him. Volokov was bigger than Juneau and even bigger than his father had been.

"Thank you for bringing her back," Volokov said, staring at him, emanating power.

"I couldn't let her be hurt. She's an innocent, and Juneau only knows how to take what he wants." He squirmed under the intense gaze and then straightened up and met it head-on. His father used to do that, and Fredrik had had much more to fear of him than he did of Mikael Volokov. After all, he was the one who just brought his niece back safe and sound.

"You have some strength in you."

"Uncle Mikael, he killed a wolf to save me," Jane explained as she stood next to her uncle. "They had tied me up, and this Juneau guy...." She shivered, and Alpha Volokov put his arm around her. "He wanted to...." She faltered.

"I think your uncle understands," Fredrik said. "And you were very brave. You thought clearly and helped me get you out of the house. You should be proud of yourself."

A woman best described as an Amazon approached Jane and folded her in her arms. "I was so worried."

"I'm sorry I went off alone. I was only going to the store for Gran, and...."

"It's all right. You thought, the way we all did, that the threat had been neutralized and we could go on with our lives the way we wanted," Mikael said. "We know that isn't so any longer, and we'll all be much more careful." It was clear from his expression that the topic wasn't over, but that he didn't want to discuss it here. "We'll talk once your mother stops fussing over you and will let you out of her sight. I figure you'll be eighteen by then."

Jane rolled her eyes, but she held tightly to her mother and alpha. "Can we go home?"

"We certainly can, baby girl." A wolf who Fredrick suspected was Jane's father guided her away from the other two and immediately folded her in his arms and simply hugged her. There were no words. Then Jane seemed to allow herself to go to pieces.

"Come back with us. The pack owes you a large debt. We had been trying to find her for a few hours when she called," Mikael said.

Fredrik hesitated. "I need to put as much distance between me and my brother as I can. I killed one of his best friends and cronies in order to get her out of there." He took a deep breath, his mind racing over everything he'd done in the last few hours. He really wanted to run and hide somewhere; that was his instinct. Fighting for what he wanted wasn't something he usually did. He was smaller than other wolves, so flight was his usual method of escaping danger, and he'd never been in more danger than he was right now.

"What you need is a chance to eat, rest, and think," Alpha Volokov said sternly. He was clearly a wolf who wasn't used to argument, and yet there was a kindness and reasonableness mixed with the strength that Fredrik nearly missed because he wasn't used to hearing it, at least not from other wolves. "In the morning we'll take you where you want to go." Mikael turned to the others. "Let's head back to the compound. Karl," he called, and a strong wolf with a grin plastered on his face jogged over. "Is this your truck?" the alpha asked Fredrik, and he shook his head.

"It was the only vehicle there. It belonged to the wolf I killed...." The enormity of what he'd done hit him like a brick wall. He'd killed someone. He had never done that before. Without thinking or caring, he'd stuck a knife in Dimitri's neck and watched him bleed out.

"Okay. Karl, take someone with you, drive the truck away, and park it in one of the tourist lots. It's going to rain tonight, so that should confuse the scents, as will hundreds of humans in the morning."

Fredrik reached into his pocket and reluctantly withdrew the keys. That truck was his chance at freedom, and he didn't want to let it go. "How...?" It seemed he was trading captivity with his brother for captivity with another pack, and there was fuck all he could do about it.

"Your brother will track you by the truck, and we want to lead him as far away from us and you as possible. Like I said, in the morning we'll help you get wherever you want to go. The airport is probably your best bet."

Fredrik handed the keys to Karl, who whistled, and one of the other wolves hurried over. They talked briefly and then took off in the truck and a car. Fredrik knew the alpha was probably right, but he hated to see the truck go.

"Everyone, let's get back to the compound," Alpha Volokov called, and the pack members moved toward the other vehicles. It was a tight squeeze, but everyone got in. Fredrik wasn't sure where he should ride, but Alpha Volokov motioned to the front of a Volvo wagon, so he got inside.

"Was Anton really your papa?" a boy of about eight asked from the backseat, sitting next to his brother, Fredrik guessed.

"He was, but he was never much of one," Fredrik answered honestly.

"He was a bad wolf," the pup said.

Fredrik turned. The pup had his arms crossed over his chest as though he were daring anyone to argue with him.

"Alexi. Fredrik is a guest," the alpha corrected him gently.

"Okay, Alpha Mikael. But Anton was still bad."

"I take it you're an alpha in training," Fredrik said to Alexi, who nodded and kept his expression serious.

"He is." Alpha Volokov kept looking over at him as he drove, probably keeping an eye on him.

"My father was mean and cruel to everyone," Fredrik said to little Alexi. "I guess I was lucky because I had a mother who wasn't like that."

"Anton defeated Alexi and Misha's father in a challenge," Alpha Volokov explained, and Fredrik nodded. He'd met plenty of wolves who felt as Alexi did.

"I'm sorry," Fredrik said to both boys. He was at a loss for words otherwise. What did you say to the pups of someone your asshole father killed in his blind rampage for power? Hallmark sure as fuck didn't make a card for that.

"We live with Alpha Mikael now," Misha said. "He's like our papa, but he isn't our papa. Not really. So is Alpha Denton."

Fredrik wasn't sure what to say about anything. He sat silently and just rode, wondering what he'd gotten himself into.

When Alpha Volokov turned, the road got rougher for a few miles, and then they turned once again and parked in front of a large, rustically sided house. The other cars and trucks pulled in behind them. Everyone piled out, and more wolves joined in the celebration.

"All right," a female voice said, cutting through the din. "I have plenty of food. Let's all go inside." She had to be the alpha's mother.

Wolves filed inside, and Fredrik got out of the way. Alpha Volokov remained behind, and a wolf almost as large joined him. They stood close together. They weren't talking to each other, but they seemed to be communicating. How he knew that, he wasn't sure; maybe it was the way they stared at each other.

Fredrik turned away when the men embraced and then kissed—hard. Arousal and the scent of passion filled the night. Fredrik stepped back at their intensity. He tried not to become aroused himself, knowing they would be able to scent it. The last thing he wanted was to come between two Alpha mates.

"Fredrik," Alpha Volokov called after they broke apart. The two of them stood together, still touching each other as though they needed it. Fredrik wondered what having someone like that would be like. "This is Denton, my mate. Denton, Fredrik rescued Jane from his brother."

Fredrik shook the much bigger wolf's hand. "I'm sorry my bloodline has caused you and yours so much trouble."

Both of them stared at him. "That's an interesting phrase," Alpha Denton said.

"I know. You would use the term family. Except what kind of family do you think my father had? It wasn't a family. More like a pack of hyenas, each after what they could get for themselves and always scouting around for someone they could use." He stepped back. "Look, if you'll tell me where you want me to stay, I'll go there and get out of everyone's way. And if you could arrange to get me to the nearest airport, I'll get a flight somewhere and be out of your hair as fast as I can."

"Come on," Alpha Denton said, motioning to the door.

When Fredrik went inside, he stopped as everyone burst into applause. He looked behind him, and then Jane, now dressed in her own clothes, took his hand and pulled him forward.

16

"You're a hero. You saved me." She actually leaned in and kissed him on the cheek, and a cheer went up once again.

Fredrik blushed fiercely and tried to figure out how he could get out of there. This was way more than what he deserved. Yes, he'd gotten Jane away from his brother, but he'd also been able to escape himself.

"This is my mother," Jane said, directing his attention to the Amazonian woman he'd seen earlier. She had a hard stare even when she was smiling.

"We appreciate what you did."

"Everyone, let's eat before the food gets cold," Mikael called.

That seemed to be the signal, but everyone waited, staring at the bowls and platters of meat. Fredrik stepped back and waited for the others.

"You're supposed to go first," Jane told him.

"Why? I'm not important enough."

Jane stared at him. "But—"

"Don't you eat by pack rank?" Fredrik asked.

"Excuse me?" Alpha Volokov said from behind him, and Fredrik jumped slightly.

"The higher-ranking pack members eat first, and then the others follow behind. I was always the lowest-ranking member of the pack because I'm…." He looked down. "Small and not able to fight like the others. So I always got what was left."

"No," Alpha Denton said. "We don't act that way. Everyone is equal and they get what they need. Yes, Mikael and I are the alphas, but what kind of leaders would we be if we always put ourselves and what we wanted first? This is a pack, a family, not a kingdom, so go on and get something to eat." He smiled.

Fredrik nodded and did as he was told. The food smelled amazing. His stomach growled as he slowly filled his plate. One of the pups stood next to him, grinning when Fredrik looked down at him as he held his plate with both hands. "You want some of this?" He nodded, and Fredrik put some of the potato salad on his plate. Then he took some himself. The rare-grilled beef had his mouth watering and his wolf salivating. He took a piece and gave the pup some as well. He kept smiling, and on second look, he recognized him as the pup from the car, the one who'd been quieter. "Are you Misha?"

"Yes, sir," he said. "Can I have some corn too?"

"I'll help him," a pretty woman said as she hurried over.

"It's okay. We got to know each other a little in the car." Fredrik pointed to the macaroni, and Misha nodded.

"Thank you," Misha said and hurried away to find a place to sit.

Fredrik turned to find an out-of-the-way place for himself. There was a chair near one of the corners, so he sat there, eating quickly.

Conversations between people who knew and cared deeply for one another went on all around him. When he was half done with his food, a group of pups in wolf form raced through the room and ended up in a happy pile.

"Pups," Alpha Volokov said gently as he opened the door, and they took off outside. "Stay close." He got yips in response as he closed the door.

Fredrik tried to remember being that happy and carefree. The sad thing was, he really couldn't. Even at that age, his father had held sway over everything and everyone.

He returned to his dinner and was just finishing when the most amazing scent curled around him, drawing him in like the heat from a flame in the middle of winter. Fredrik looked around, sniffing the air multiple times, trying to figure out where that smell was coming from, but he saw no one new, and it didn't seem as though anyone had joined the group. He set his plate aside and followed the scent while trying not to look as though he was tracking game, because this was so much better than that. His heart beat a little faster and sweat beaded on his forehead. His eyes shifted to seeing black and white, and his canines descended.

Fredrik had no idea what was happening to him, but he hadn't lost control of his wolf since he was ten years old and his brother Cass had nearly killed him. His father had been so proud of Cass that he'd taken him away and left Fredrik to try to shift to heal himself. It had

18

taken him hours, and he'd needed the help of his mother to keep from getting stuck in his wolf form.

The scent dissipated. Fredrik's eyes returned to seeing normal and his teeth retracted. He took a deep breath to clear the fog from his head.

"The truck is all taken care of," Karl said, clapping Fredrik on the back. "You know, you're a hero."

Fredrik shook his head. "I'm just a guy who did what was right."

"No. Good people don't do what is right all the time. It takes courage to do what you did." A large wolf said as he approached.

"That's Kaiawa," Karl explained. "We're Mikael and Denton's betas."

"It's good to meet you. I'm Fredrik." He shook Kaiawa's hand. "I'm pretty much a nobody. The only reason I had any status in my pack was because of my father."

Kaiawa leaned a little closer, and Fredrik knew he was smelling him. "You aren't an omega. But you aren't a nobody either." He turned to glance at the alphas and then his deep eyes fell on Fredrik once again.

"Thank God I'm not an omega. My father had no use for them and harassed his last one until he went out of his mind. Everything an omega is seemed to rub my father the wrong way. He didn't want peace in his pack, but vigilance, and he felt the best way to achieve that was to make sure everyone was always on their toes, doing exactly what he wanted."

"Well, like I said, you are not a nobody." Kaiawa moved away, and Karl seemed to follow him with his gaze.

"He's very different, but he speaks the truth. A nobody would never have risked his life for Jane."

This was one of the strangest conversations Fredrik had ever had. He knew his place in his pack—or his former pack. They didn't care about him other than for what he might be able to do for them. There was none of the mutual care and understanding that seemed to flow from this group like water. "Thank you." He wasn't sure what else to say. He'd spent years in an environment where he'd been beaten down, and a few kind words—and he knew that was all they were—weren't going to change how he saw himself. He'd saved someone they cared about, and that was all.

"Have you had enough to eat? You look like you haven't gotten a square meal in years, and if I know Mom, she'd like nothing better than the chance to fatten you up," Karl said.

"I've had plenty." He smiled. "Alpha Volokov said he had a place I can stay for the night and that tomorrow someone would take me where I wanted to go. I thought I'd go out east and get as far as I can from my brother. I heard there's a pack outside Asheville, so maybe I can try my luck there."

"Of course. We have a guest cabin. Well, a new guest cabin. Anna, Alexi, and Misha live in what used to be the old one. You probably met the little balls of energy."

"He did," a pretty woman, very pregnant, said, and then she smiled warmly at Karl.

"This is my mate, Mattie." He looked about as proud as any expectant father could possibly be.

"I'm going to go home and put my feet up. I'm starting to feel like my wolf is going to take over." She smiled slightly. "I'm having twins, and it feels like more than two. My wolf thinks we're having an entire litter, and she's been pounding at me to let her out, which I can't do while I'm pregnant, so…."

"I can take you back if you want," Karl said so gently that Fredrik turned away to give them some privacy.

"I'll be fine." She lightly touched Fredrik's shoulder. "It's all right. Everyone around here is fairly open about their feelings for one another. You'll find that affection is part of everyday life."

"That's something I know nothing about."

"If you stay, you will," Mattie said and then waddled slowly toward the back of the house.

He heard the door open, and the delicious aroma from earlier wafted in on the night breeze. Before he could stop himself, Fredrik followed the scent, but it dissipated when he stepped outside. When the breeze came up, rustling the trees, he caught it again, calling its siren song.

"Is there someone out here?" Fredrik called into the darkness. He usually had very good night vision, but the lights of the compound were making it difficult for him to see.

"You probably saw Mikael's brother, Christopher," Jane's mother said. "I'm Catherine, and I wanted to thank you again for all you did for my daughter. I don't know what any of us would have done…."

"I'm glad I could help her." Catherine made him nervous. He could feel the power radiating off her and guessed that being helpless to protect her daughter had taken a toll on her.

"I am in your debt."

"You owe me nothing," Fredrik said.

Catherine clapped him on the shoulder, catching his gaze and holding it. "That changes nothing. I am in your debt regardless, and I always make good. My children, mate, and pack are the center of my life."

"Then tell me about Christopher," Fredrik said, scenting as quietly as possible, desperate to catch another whiff of heaven.

"He came home from college almost a year ago, but hasn't been able to find his place in the pack. Christopher and Mikael argued over how the pack should be run, and again after Christopher requested that Mikael put him up to lead one of the packs that's reforming after—" Catherine paused.

"My father's defeat. You can say it. I have no illusions as to who and what he was."

"Christopher wished to lead one of the packs, but Mikael believes that leadership needs to form naturally, and Christopher isn't an alpha, even though he might wish he were. He also isn't beta or strong enough to be an enforcer. So he thinks he's stuck and has spent most of his time alone on the edges of the pack. He says he's trying to figure things out."

Fredrik understood how Christopher might feel even though he'd never met him. "I never fit in either."

"Maybe that's a good thing for all of us. If you had fit in, then you might not have had the conscience to do what you did. I was lucky. My place in the pack and family were always evident. But sometimes we need to look harder to figure out where we fit in. I think that's what Christopher is trying to do, but I doubt he's going to come up with the answer by living alone. You can't fit into a group or a pack if you hold yourself separate from it." She raised her voice, and the last part of the speech most definitely wasn't for Fredrik's benefit.

"I was told I could use the guest cabin, but I'm not sure where that is."

Catherine nodded. "It's right over there. Just go on in and make yourself comfortable. If you need anything, just let us know." She smiled, and Fredrik thanked her before heading toward the cabin and a place to rest.

CHAPTER 2

CHRISTOPHER VOLOKOV stood at the edge of the wooded compound, drawn by a scent unlike anything he'd ever experienced before. After four years away at college, where his wolf had been forced to hide nearly all the time, his wolf had gotten more and more demanding. So when he returned to his pack, Christopher's wolf side had taken over. The others hadn't understood at all. He'd argued with his alpha and brother Mikael and fought with others in the pack simply because he was frustrated and his wolf wanted what he wanted. For the past few months, he'd stayed away and only came around for monthly runs. But then, in the morning, he'd return to the small cave where he'd been living. He knew this behavior had to stop or his wolf would want to remain in control all the time.

That was already a danger. Christopher rocked from foot to foot as he watched the stranger step out of the pack house and walk across the compound. He seemed to be scenting the air, looking for something. Christopher did the same, wondering what the unknown wolf wanted.

At that moment the wind blew over him toward the stranger, and he stopped instantly, looking in Christopher's direction. "I know you're there."

Christopher had little doubt of that. It wasn't as though he could miss the stranger's scent. The wind shifted, and Christopher's head spun the way his friends described how they'd felt when they smoked some weed. He'd tried it, but the stuff did nothing for him except make him cough and his wolf feel sick.

He closed his eyes, relishing the headiness that washed over him. He had no idea what it meant or its exact source, but he took a step closer and then one more as he rode the intricately woven ribbons of earthy musk strung through the air. They were so intense Christopher could almost see them, like strings of multicolored sensory waves that danced and undulated through the air.

Then the breeze stopped and the air grew very still. The delight he'd reveled in disappeared, and Christopher blinked as he came out of his haze. He stepped back, wondering just what had happened to him. He knew he should retreat to the woods and his cave, but his wolf sat up, tail wagging, on alert and ready to pounce in the best way possible.

The stranger took a few tentative steps in his direction.

"Alpha Mikael asked me to show you the way." Little Alexi bounded up to the stranger and skidded to a stop. "He said he saw you out here and thought you might need help."

"I do, thank you." The stranger followed Alexi across to the far side of the compound.

Christopher retreated farther into the darkness the trees provided, but he kept his eyes on them as they walked.

"Did your papa really kill my papa in a challenge?" Alexi asked.

"I'm afraid he did," the stranger answered.

Christopher's mouth dropped open. This stranger was one of Anton's sons. Mikael must know that if Alexi did. What the hell was he doing here?

"I'm not like my father, and I'm sorry you lost your papa. I don't know what else to tell you except that my father wasn't a good man."

"Misha and I have Alpha Mikael and Alpha Denton now, and our mama."

They kept walking farther away, and Christopher couldn't stop himself from trailing them, like this stranger was the Pied Piper. The breeze blew toward him in a direct line, and within seconds Christopher's skin pricked and his eyes watered. He ached to race toward the stranger.

He gripped the tree in front of him, bark biting into his skin. He didn't know what was happening. Part of him wanted the stranger more than he'd wanted anyone in his life, and his logical half had no fucking idea what was happening. His cock ached and stood straight out from his body. He'd traveled here in his wolf form and shifted a while ago, but he needed to resist and let his human side retain some control.

"You know, you're really lucky," the stranger said. "Alpha Mikael is a good leader, and he's a nice man. My father was my alpha, and he was nothing like Alpha Mikael."

"He was a bad wolf," Alexi said, his voice growing softer but still carrying to Christopher's sensitive ears.

"Yes, he was."

The door to the guest cabin opened, and the stranger said good night to Alexi and then closed the door. The delicious scent that had filled the night with wonder and happiness was snuffed out like a candle.

Alexi shifted and then bounded back toward the main house, skittering around the chairs in the central area. He yipped at the glass door, and it slid open, allowing Alexi back inside with the rest of the pack.

Christopher looked toward the pack house and then over at the guest cabin. He figured he could join the rest of the pack if he wanted. He wasn't sure how happy they'd be to see him, but he was family. Instead, he turned and crept closer to the guest cabin and then shifted into wolf form, his bones cracking as they reconfigured in a matter of seconds.

Instantly the forest came alive. He heard little creatures skittering under the leaves and rustling in the trees above him. Squirrels, rabbits, mice, even an owl as it landed above—all of it as clear to his wolf as if he'd seen it. He could also see between the trees to where the guest cabin light came on. Without thinking, he prowled closer and found a slight indentation in the earth. He lay down, gaze glued to the building that held the stranger, watching and waiting—for what, he wasn't sure.

Eventually the lights went off inside, but Christopher stayed where he was, watching. The others eventually drifted back to their homes, talking and laughing as they went, but he stayed still.

You don't have to do this. You know you are perfectly welcome to rejoin the pack.

His brother stood next to him, a huge wolf towering over him. In his wolf form, Christopher couldn't speak, of course, and he hadn't been given the ability to speak directly to the minds of other wolves the way his brother could. Hell, there were many things his brother got that he never did.

This is still your family and pack. Don't you think it's time you stopped all this and rejoined the rest of us?

Christopher shook his head.

Not all of us are happy with our lot in life. But we all either live with it or make the changes required in our lives so we can be happy. You can't be happy like this, all alone all the time. It isn't how wolves are happy.

How could he explain to his brother that all he wanted was something of his own? Someplace that belonged only to him. His brother was the alpha. Yeah, he had Denton, who everyone also called alpha, but it was Mikael who was the stronger wolf and ultimately the one in charge. This was his pack, and he made the decisions and plans. Everyone else was happy with that.

You have talents that will benefit the pack. That's why we sent you to college.

Christopher glanced at his brother, then turned back to the guest cabin and rested his chin on the ground so he could still watch.

Do you think it was just us who allowed you to go? The pack sent you. All of us did without so you could go. Each and every member helped you. I know you don't think so, but you owe all of them a lot, and part of how you can begin to repay them is not to act like a spoiled child. You're a wolf and a full member of this pack.

Christopher lifted his head and nodded. He knew Mikael was right. In a pack, everyone supported everyone else, and he'd been away for four years and hadn't wanted for anything. His tuition, room, board, books—all of it was paid… for what? So he could mope around here because everything wasn't the way he wanted it to be? He wanted to tell his brother that he'd try, but when he turned back toward him, he was alone. The thing that drove him crazy was that Mikael was the only wolf he knew who ever had the ability to sneak up on him—no sound, no scent. It was unnerving.

Just rejoin the pack and we can figure out the rest. It's time you came back to your family.

The other fucking thing he hated was the way Mikael could talk to everyone just by putting his thoughts in their mind.

I know you hate when I do this, but I wouldn't bother if I didn't care. There was a brief pause. *I know why you're lying outside in the dark, probably wondering what's going on. Come see me in the morning, dressed and in human form. We'll talk.* His brother chuckled, and then there was silence.

Christopher huffed and closed his eyes. Maybe if he was still and quiet, his brother would leave him alone. He waited a few minutes, but it seemed his brother had said what he wanted to say while asserting that he could find Christopher pretty much whenever he wanted.

It also figured that Mikael would know and understand what was happening to him. Christopher knew he wasn't an alpha because true alpha wolves had gifts that allowed them to be good leaders and keep their pack members safe. Mikael had all those gifts. He seemed to know instinctively when someone was in trouble or in need. Just like he'd come to him—Mikael just knew.

Christopher had none of those gifts, and damned if he could figure out what he was good at. Yeah, he'd done well in school and worked hard, but how could philosophy, history, and the other classes he'd taken help him or his pack way out here? He had also taken business classes, but the pack mostly lived off what they could produce or make themselves. The few classes he'd taken when thinking of becoming a veterinarian might be the most useful. They were wolves and lived close to the land, so as far as he was concerned, he had nothing to contribute, and very little status other than being the alpha's brother....

Christopher decided the best thing to do was to go to sleep and figure things out in the morning. He thought about going back to his cave, but he was drawn to the stranger in the guest cabin, so he curled into a ball to keep the cool evening air at bay and went to sleep.

SOMETHING LANDED on top of him, and Christopher went instantly on alert. High-pitched growls followed. Thankfully, Christopher recognized his nephew, William, and his friends Alexi and Misha. They growled and pounced on him, playing. Christopher got to his feet and gently knocked one of the pups aside. Misha jumped on his back again, and Christopher allowed the three of them to bring him down. Soon they were all rolling on the ground.

"Boys, let Uncle Christopher wake up."

The boys stopped and stood, blinking up at Catherine, clearly not happy at having their game stopped.

"Mama," William said after shifting. "We were just playing pounce, the way Alpha Mikael does." The others shifted as well, and soon three naked boys stood staring up at Christopher's intimidating sister.

"Did you ask first?"

"No, Mama. He was an antelope. You don't tell the antelope that you're hunting him." William rolled his eyes, and if Christopher had been in his human form, he would have had to cover his mouth to keep from laughing. As it was, his wolf did a decent imitation that earned a glare from his sister.

Christopher nudged William and then turned and loped off through the woods, thankful the pups didn't follow. Once he was out of sight, he picked up speed and raced to the cave. Once inside, he shifted and dressed. In the pack, members came and went all the time, so nudity was nothing unusual, but it was a good idea when summoned by your alpha to appear dressed and as though you took the meeting seriously.

By the time he returned to the compound and approached the main house, the scent from the night before was back, intensifying the closer he got. Christopher pulled open the door to the pack lodge and stepped inside as the urge to shift and race through toward the source of that scent nearly overpowered him.

"Sweetheart," his mother said, hugging him and looking him over. "Have you spent too much time with your wolf? Your teeth and—" She paused and her eyes widened. "Honey, that's so wonderful." She grinned and began gushing.

"What are you talking about?" He was hard enough to pound nails and figured his mother could smell his arousal, but he hoped to God she didn't want to talk about it. Very few things embarrassed him; after all, he'd awakened to the sight of three naked boys standing in front of his sister, explaining he was the antelope in their game. After that, there wasn't much that could embarrass anyone, except maybe his mother asking why he was sporting a stiffie.

"There you are," Mikael said as he came in, carrying a mug. He kissed their mother on the cheek. "Leave him alone for now, Mom. You can gush over him later." Mikael motioned toward the stairs, and Christopher realized Mikael meant for them to go up to his studio.

He nodded and sighed, following Mikael up to the top of the house. Christopher always loved the view from this room, though he'd never spent much time in it because most of the time it was off limits as Mikael's workroom.

"Have you decided it's time to rejoin the pack?"

"I never left the pack. I just needed some time to figure things out."

"And what did you learn?" Mikael asked. He pulled up one of his stools and sat on it, sipping from his mug.

"I don't know. That I don't fit in no matter what I do, so I might as well not try."

"Bullshit," Mikael said in full rumbly alpha voice. "What do you want to do?"

"I wanted to lead the reformed Greenview pack," Christopher said.

"And I told you then that you weren't qualified. No one in the pack will follow you. You aren't big enough or a strong enough leader. They were torn apart by Anton, and most of the members were traumatized by years under his thumb. That pack is trying to heal and move on. They needed someone who went through all that

29

with them and came out strong enough to both lead and help. That wasn't you." Mikael drank some more of his coffee. "I think you know that."

"But I'm your brother."

Mikael slid off the stool and stalked over to him. "If you think I'm going to treat you any differently than I treat anyone else, you're crazy. Catherine and Karl have earned their spots in the pack, and so did Kaiawa. If you want a leadership role, then you need to fight for it. No one is going to hand you one." Mikael sighed. "That isn't why we're here."

"No?" Christopher put his hands on his hips, staring directly at his brother.

"Are you challenging me?" Mikael asked, and with a single movement and before Christopher could flinch, Mikael shifted his hand and had it at his throat, claws scraping his skin. "I'm your alpha, and you will act like it."

Christopher swallowed and leaned his head to the side, shifting his gaze away.

Mikael pulled his hand away, and it was human once again before it settled at his side. "You need to show respect for me, and for others in the pack. Otherwise you will never fit in or be accepted. The pack is your family, and if you respect and support them, they will do the same for you. And I'm willing to bet that all the things you want will fall into place."

"Yes, Alpha," Christopher said, still reeling at the power his brother wielded with what seemed like such ease.

"Good. Now, do you want to tell me why I found you in the woods outside the guest cabin last night?"

"I couldn't stay away," Christopher answered. "I was drawn there."

"Of course you were." Mikael set his mug aside.

"Why do you say that?" Christopher asked, but Mikael only smiled at him and seemed to be waiting him out. Christopher paused a few minutes, and then his teeth elongated and everything went black and white. That scent from last night assaulted him and damn near made Christopher's knees buckle. His entire body thrummed, and he wanted desperately to get out of the room. "I need to go."

"No. You need very much to stay where you are. You aren't about to lose control of your wolf the way you think you are."

A knock sounded on the door, and Mikael opened it. The stranger from the night before stopped in the doorway, mirroring the near exact expression Christopher knew he had to be wearing. Up close, the stranger was gorgeous, with jet-black hair and eyes, a full mouth, olive skin, and a scent Christopher knew came directly from heaven. That was the only possible explanation.

"This is Fredrik. He saved Jane and returned her to us."

Christopher nodded, not really listening. He couldn't take his eyes off Fredrik. Christopher took a step closer. He wanted to take Fredrik in his arms, guide him out of the house and back to the guest cabin, lock the door, and take him right there on the floor. "I'm Christopher." Damn, his chest was tight, and getting enough air into his lungs was difficult. He closed his eyes and forced a deep breath.

"Do you know what's happening?" Fredrik asked.

Christopher looked at Mikael and then back to Fredrik. "I think we're mates." As soon as he said the words, he knew they were true and instantly felt better. Well, at least he could breathe a little more as he took in his mate and how gorgeous he was.

Fredrik shivered and his black eyes widened.

Christopher hurried forward without a second thought and pulled Fredrik to him, putting himself between Fredrik and his brother. He turned to Mikael and growled. "He's mine."

"I figured as much," Mikael said calmly.

"Why didn't you say something?" Christopher growled again. Finding one's mate was the dream of each and every wolf, but it didn't always happen.

"I knew you'd figure it out for yourself." Mikael finished his coffee. "Now, why don't the two of you go someplace where you can be alone and talk things out?" He chuckled. "Instinct is going to try very hard to take over, and both your wolves want to go at each other tooth and nail."

Christopher nodded. He definitely wanted to find a bed, like right now.

"I suggest you talk to each other before having sex or completing your mate bond."

"We're mates. What is there to talk about?" Christopher asked, turning to Fredrik.

"Um… I'm leaving. I need to get out of the area and away from my brother."

Christopher released him and stepped back.

"See? I'm not the alpha for nothing," Mikael said. "You need to talk to one another before you bind your lives together. It's very important that your human as well as your wolf is happy."

Christopher nodded and left the room, then descended the stairs without saying another word. He'd actually found his mate, and he was leaving. Well, didn't that just figure?

"Where are you going?" Fredrik asked from behind him as his light footsteps tread the stairs.

"Back to my cave in the woods. I think that's where I'm best off." He wasn't going to explain that he felt like his heart had been found and then ripped away. "You can go where you need to, and I'll do my best to try to forget we ever met." After all, how hard could it be to push from your mind someone you'd known for exactly five minutes?

"But…."

Christopher reached the main floor. He hoped he could go out the back door and directly to the woods. He could shift and take off. But, of course, he ran into his mother, who was grinning proudly.

"You found your mate?" she asked.

"Yeah, and he's leaving, so what good does it do?"

"Don't speak to Mom like that," Mikael snapped from behind him, and Christopher groaned. All he wanted to do was get out of here. "I said that you should talk to him, and I meant it." Mikael caught his attention and then looked at Fredrik, who seemed to be trying to melt into the wall. "You have more important things to worry about than your own problems and hurt feelings."

Christopher knew his brother was right. He walked to Fredrik and gently took his hand. He brought it to his nose and inhaled deeply. His head swam. "Do you want to talk? We can go to your cabin."

"Okay," Fredrik said barely above a whisper.

Christopher still held Fredrik's hand, loving how it felt in his. The common area outside was filled with activity—pups running, pack members repairing buildings, and even what might have been a few furniture projects in progress—but he barely noticed any of it.

He opened the door, and once Fredrik was inside, he closed it and pulled Fredrik into his arms, taking the first taste of his mate's lips. Everything that a few seconds earlier had seemed wrong with his world didn't matter anymore. Fredrik tasted amazing, perfect, and exactly the way Christopher had always dreamed his mate would taste. He even made a small groan that sent flame shooting down Christopher's spine.

"I thought we were supposed to talk," Fredrik said, pulling away.

"Kiss now, talk later," he proposed and leaned in again. This time he held Fredrik tighter, cupping his head in his hand, deepening the kiss until he could hardly see or think straight. His wolf wanted to tug all of Fredrik's clothes off and see if his mate tasted just as good everywhere else. His cock throbbed at that thought, and Christopher slid one hand down Fredrik's back, cupped his ass, and pressed their hips together. Fredrik was as excited as he was. He moaned softly as Christopher slipped his tongue between his lips. Christopher had always loved kissing, but this was better than any kiss he'd ever had, and to think it was their first one—well, second if you counted the break. Not that it really mattered, because he wasn't going to keep count. God, he was rambling in his head. Fredrik must have scrambled his brains.

"Christopher," Fredrik whimpered and held his shoulders, pushing away slightly. "We need to talk. That's why we're here. Remember?"

"Actually, I don't remember anything from before I kissed you. Everything is a blur."

Fredrik laughed, a gentle warm sound that made Christopher lean closer once again. "Christopher. We have to talk." He sounded jittery, and the stress cut through the cloud of desire that had engulfed Christopher's mind. "I got Jane away from my brother, but to do that, I had to kill one of his cronies. He isn't going to stop looking for me. That's why I have to leave. I have to put as much distance between him and me as I can." Fredrik shook in Christopher's arms. "There's no way he'll stop looking for me, and it won't take him very long to figure out that I returned his 'present' to her pack, and then this will be the first place he looks."

"Excuse me?" Christopher asked. "My cousin was some sort of present for your brother?" He was mortified.

"Yeah. Dimitri, the guy I killed, grabbed her and brought her back to my brother. He'd have had his fun with her, and then Jane would have disappeared, I'm sure. I got the feeling that Dimitri and Yuri had done something like this before. My brother is hypersexual, even for a wolf, so he thinks nothing of using anyone he can and then discarding them. He inherited that trait from my father."

"Jesus. How does anyone in the pack survive?"

"By keeping their heads low, preferably out of his sight. I know pack members who tried to hide their daughters from my father so he wouldn't decide that he wanted them. People were property to my father, and my brother is turning out the same way. All he wants is to return to how things were under my father. And your brother is the center of all his attention."

"Do you think he knew who Jane was?"

"Yes, but I don't think he cared."

Christopher nodded, his mind already racing. "We need to talk to Mikael. He has to know this."

"I already told him this morning," Fredrik said.

"What did he say?"

"He said that if I wanted to stay here in the pack, he would welcome me. He said that as far as he and the pack were concerned, anyone who was willing to put themselves on the line for a member of the pack deserved the pack's protection."

"That sounds like Mikael, and he means it," Christopher said. "Mikael never says anything he doesn't mean. He's all about integrity and treating others the way they should be treated. He's a great alpha." As soon as he said the words, he knew they were true. He had been giving Mikael grief, or at least blaming Mikael for not giving him what he wanted. But finding his place in the pack was his own responsibility, not Mikael's. Christopher's mind had taken a little trip, and he pulled his attention back to the conversation at hand.

"That may be. But I can't stay here and put all of you at risk."

Christopher scoffed. "This is the safest place for you. Old Faithful is the strongest pack in this part of the country, and Mikael has the loyalty and support of every other pack alpha in this area. They owe him their allegiance and loyalty." Christopher wanted him to stay; there was no doubt about it. Two days ago he'd had no idea that Fredrik existed, but as soon as he smelled him and held him in his arms—his mate, the one person destined to be his—he knew he couldn't just let him go.

"I can't." Fredrik pulled away. "I know we only get one mate, but the timing of this just sucks. If I'd have met you a few days ago, even a week or month ago, I'd have come here and I would have been able to be happy about it."

"But we're mates," Christopher said. "We're supposed to try." They hadn't even had an hour together. Was that all the time he was going to get with his mate? "I could go with you."

Fredrik paused and then shook his head. "You need to be with your family. Yours is actually worth being around. They support one another and care about what happens to one another. Mikael cares what happens to you and everyone in the pack."

"But I don't fit in here."

"Yes, you do." Fredrik slumped a little. "I haven't been loved since my mother died five years ago. She took care of me and made sure I knew what it felt like to be loved. No one else in my father's pack cared. They were all trying to survive my father's psychotic leadership, or they were part of it and did their best to get everything they could, either by sucking up to my father or stepping on those weaker than them. It was hell. This pack is heaven compared to them. I know that and I've been here less than a day."

"Then stay, at least for a while." Christopher would accept him giving it a try.

"The longer I'm here, the more likely it is that Juneau will find me," Fredrik said, even as Christopher saw the longing in his eyes. Fredrik seemed to have wished for a pack like the one Christopher had taken for granted for years.

"Then the pack will protect you. It's what real packs do. They stand together when times get hard and work as a team to make the most of it when times are good." Not that he'd been doing that for the past year. That had to change, and if he was lucky, he'd have the chance to do that with his mate by his side. "At least talk to Mikael." Christopher could hardly believe, after giving his brother worry and grief for months, he was finally figuring out that Mikael had been right all along. Dang, he hated when that happened.

"I don't know."

"At least try for me and for the chance to be mates. I was always told that finding your mate was the greatest thing that could happen to a wolf, though I never believed it."

"But you do now? You don't know anything about me. What if I'm exactly like my brother… deep down? What if as hard as I try not to be, I'm still like my father and all that is just waiting to come out?"

Christopher knew that wasn't true. There was nothing like that in his mate. "I don't think so."

"How can you know?"

"The Mother gives us what we need in a mate. We wouldn't get someone we weren't supposed to be with. I wasn't here when Mikael met Denton. I came home after all the excitement was over, but they brought two packs together and made them stronger. Mikael was always strong, but now he's happy, contented, and even stronger because he always has Denton to guard his back. No matter what."

"He has betas for that."

"Well, the betas guard his physical back, and Denton does that too, but I think Denton also has Mikael's emotional back. That's what I want with my mate. Someone who will always be there for me, and I can be there for them."

Fredrik sighed. "Are you really sure about this? You could be biting off a lot more than you or anyone here is expecting."

"From the stories I heard, Anton tried to burn out Denton's pack, and they even tried to take him. He was relentless in what he tried to do to Mikael and Denton. They stood up to him and ultimately took him down." Christopher let some pride creep into his voice and then remembered he was talking about Fredrik's father. Granted, there seemed to be no love lost between them, but it still had to be hard knowing so many people hated him.

Fredrik swallowed and closed his eyes. "I'll stay for a few days and try to keep out of sight. I can hope that Juneau finds the truck and thinks I took off."

"Is there anyone you trust who could maybe spread a little disinformation?" Christopher asked as he grinned to beat the band. Before Fredrik could answer, Christopher pulled him into another kiss. He didn't want to talk about all this at the moment. Hell, he didn't want to talk at all. He had gotten what he wanted, for now at least, and he planned to make the very most of it.

"Maybe," Fredrik answered when he pulled away from the kiss.

Christopher laughed. "How can you keep your mind on track after a kiss like that? All I can think about is you."

"If you grew up the way I did, you'd learn never to be distracted by anything or anyone. My pack members often hunted in pairs. And they didn't necessarily hunt game, if you know what I mean."

That was pretty sick.

Christopher lifted Fredrik off his feet, and Fredrik fought him for a few seconds. He held Fredrik tight and ran his hands down to his butt, supporting him once Fredrik stopped squirming and wound his arms around Christopher's neck. Once it was safe to move, Christopher walked Fredrik over to the bed, kissing him the entire time. He could feel and smell his future mate's fear, though not of him. It was lower grade, not immediate, but the stressful kind of fear when you aren't sure about what will happen. "I'm going to do my very best to distract you, because I don't want you thinking about anyone but me."

"You think you can do that?" Fredrik asked as Christopher laid him on the bed.

"Oh yeah," he smirked and pulled off Fredrik's shirt. He tugged a little too hard and the fabric ripped in his hands.

"Hey," Fredrik said.

"Sorry." He tossed what was left of the shirt aside and raked his gaze down Fredrik's richly warm skin. Dang, he was trim, with faint lines on his belly, and pink-brown nipples that pebbled perfectly under Christopher's fingers. "Damn, you're even prettier than I imagined." He leaned forward and captured a nipple between his lips. He worried the bud with his tongue and then carefully scraped it with his teeth. He didn't want to break Fredrik's skin, not yet. Things between them were way too up in the air for that. As long as they didn't complete their mating, they could step away from each other, so no matter how much his wolf urged him to mark Fredrik as his, Christopher held back.

That didn't mean he couldn't taste, and he did plenty of that. He ran his tongue down Fredrik's belly, loving the flutter of Fredrik's muscles. "You taste good, like earth and herbs mixed together, the best that the Mother has to offer."

"I don't know who this mother you're talking about is," Fredrik whimpered.

"Don't worry. She knows you, or you wouldn't have been chosen as my mate." He inhaled and his head spun. He adored Fredrik's scent, but as he continued sniffing, he detected something around the edges. It was barely there, and he wasn't sure what it was. Something, some part of Fredrik, was foreign to him, and he couldn't place what the scent was. He'd thought it was the fear he'd been sensing, but that wasn't it. It could just be one of the unique things that was part of his mate. Not that it particularly mattered at this moment.

"Okay," Fredrik said.

Dang, there went that vigilance again. Christopher sucked a line down Fredrik's belly to the waistband of his pants. He wanted to tear the fabric away, but kept his head enough to open Fredrik's belt and push the denim away. Fredrik's scent was very strong in the fabric, and Christopher figured this was the second day he'd worn them. Not that he minded in the least; he could never get enough of his mate's scent. Christopher pulled the jeans away and tugged off Fredrik's boxer briefs. He buried his face between Fredrik's legs, inhaling deeply as Fredrik quivered. "Are you excited or nervous?"

"Both."

"You never have to be nervous around me. I'll never hurt you." He ran his hands down Fredrik's legs, the light hair tickling his palms. "You're gorgeous." He flicked his tongue along Fredrik's cock, sampling before he went in for the full meal. His mate tasted even better when he sucked him in, salty richness bursting on his tongue. His wolf growled his approval, and Christopher took Fredrik deeper, needing as much of him as possible.

"Chris...," Fredrik groaned, and Christopher felt Fredrik's wolf coming very near the surface. His own wolf desperately wanted out so he could taste his mate directly, but Christopher needed to keep him under control. Right now he wanted his mate as a man—they needed to get to know each other that way. Their wolves already approved of the mating, and if they let them loose, they'd mate forever before either of them could stop it.

"I know, sweetheart," Christopher said and sucked him once more, taking him deep, burying his nose in the skin at the base of his cock, smelling his mate's intensity as he quivered and shook on the bed.

"I'm so close. It's too soon, and—"

Christopher sucked hard, desperately wanting to see his mate come. It wasn't long before he got his wish. Fredrik threw his head back, howling as Christopher took his release, swallowing every drop. As soon as Fredrik settled back on the bed, Christopher let him slip from between his lips and kissed him hard. His own cock ached between his legs and he was damn close himself, but his mate was more important. "Damn, you're hot," Christopher whispered.

"I want you," Fredrik moaned between kisses.

Christopher climbed off the bed and undressed as quickly as he possibly could. Fredrik lay on his back, his head at the edge of the bed. Fuck, that was hot, and when Fredrik parted his lips, Christopher's knees nearly buckled. He moved closer, and Fredrik guided Christopher's cock between his lips.

He rocked back and forth slowly as Fredrik sucked him hard, deep. Fuck, he was hot as all get-out. The pressure inside Christopher's head was almost too much, and watching his cock slide between Fredrik's luscious lips was nearly enough for him to come from that alone. He leaned forward, his hips undulating, and Fredrik took all of him.

Christopher put his hands on the mattress, leaning forward. He bent his neck and sucked in the head of Fredrik's cock, which had come back to life with renewed vigor. "That's it. Take all of me," Christopher whispered, stroking Fredrik's cock. "You feel so good."

Fredrik gripped him, sliding his swollen, slick lips up and down his shaft. Christopher straightened up, still stroking Fredrik, but he had to watch. His mate certainly knew exactly what he wanted and how he loved to be touched. He panted as Fredrik continued sucking him. This was mind-blowing, and soon the tingles of impending release started deep inside. His wolf was as ecstatic as he was. He felt Fredrik's teeth elongate, lightly scraping his cock, adding another layer of sensation that damn near stripped him of the last bit of control.

"Soon."

Fredrik sucked harder, sliding his hands to his ass, cupping his cheeks and pulling Christopher forward. Damn, the way he gripped him and held him there, wet heat surrounding him, made Christopher's heart race and pound in his ears. This was unbelievable. He couldn't hang on any longer and threw his head back, howling his release toward the ceiling.

When Christopher could think once again, he turned to find Fredrik smiling up at him. He'd pulled away and seemed happy as hell.

"You are so hot." Fredrik rolled over on the bed and then knelt, pulling Christopher forward. "Was that okay? I haven't done…."

"Are you a virgin?"

"No. But my brother and father didn't think very much of anyone who was gay, so I pretty much kept to myself. I was always afraid that if I got serious with anyone, word would get back to them somehow. My father always seemed to know things, and I never figured out how. I suspect he was paying my roommate to feed him information or something. So I never had a boyfriend, and what sex I did have was with guys I was sure didn't know me."

"So it was quick and unsatisfying," Christopher supplied.

"Yeah. It was that." Again Fredrik flashed his brilliant smile. "This was so different."

Christopher climbed onto the bed and pulled Fredrik to him so they were both comfortable. "I'm glad. I was told as a child that finding your mate and being with them was magical. I haven't talked to Mikael about how it is with him and Denton, but from the noise they make, especially when the windows are open, I'd say it's magical for them too." Christopher snickered. "Sometimes there are disadvantages to being a wolf. One of them is hearing your brother and his mate go at it like rabbits, and the other is that you can hear your parents when they get frisky."

"We're supposed to ignore things like that. At least that's what my mother told me. Though she could have said that to try to keep me from being traumatized by my father and all the women he had. I swear he was part goat too."

"No. We're all taught that, but some of us are better at ignoring things than others."

"Tell me about it," Catherine said from outside, and Christopher cringed as her laughter grew softer.

"I guess we need to be quieter," Fredrik said.

41

"Or find sisters who are nicer and keep their mouths shut," Christopher said loudly enough that if Catherine was in earshot, she'd get the message. Since he didn't get a reply, he assumed she was too far away.

Christopher held Fredrik for a long while, content just to spend time with his mate. He had a million questions, but hopefully over the next few days, he'd have a chance to get them answered. For now, they needed some quiet time with just the two of them.

"I think I'm going to need some more clothes," Fredrik said. "You ripped my shirt, and that was all I had. I didn't take the time to pack a bag before I left. Getting away was more important."

"I have some clothes."

"You said you were living in a cave."

"I have been for most of the past year, but Mom insisted that I keep a room at the main house. She said I might be part wolf, but that was no excuse to be living like an animal, so I have most of my clothes there."

"I like your mom. She reminds me a lot of my own mother. Mom was strong enough to stand up to my father for a while. They weren't mates or anything, thank goodness. My mother never let things get that far with my father."

"Do you think she loved him?" Christopher asked.

Fredrik shivered and moved closer to him. "What I think, though my mom never said, was that she was like Jane, a girl they got because my father wanted to have sex with as many women as possible so he could have more and more children. My mother hated my father, but she kept that to herself. She did what she could to keep my father away from me. I know she tried to leave the pack more than once, and she would have. My father even said she could go—I remember them arguing about it. But my father said I would stay with him, and my mother could never leave me." Fredrik buried his face in his shoulder.

"What is it?"

"My father wanted my mother to have more children, so he decided he was going to make it happen. He was the alpha, after all, and stronger than everyone else. She fought him off, but he hurt her, and after that, she wasn't the same. That was a few years before she died. She moved to a small house at the edge of the pack land. She said she had to be as far from him as she could get. I think that's what kept me away from my father's attention for a while. Mom and I were happy, and she insisted I study hard so I'd be able to go to college. She always said I was super smart, and that my only chance to get away was to go to school. She even got my father to agree to pay for it." Fredrik shivered again, and Christopher wondered just what she'd had to do to secure that agreement. Whatever it was, it probably hadn't been kind or pretty.

"She died, and I went away to school. I actually thought I was free of him, especially after he died, but then the money began to run out. I got a job and worked, but it wasn't enough." Fredrik sighed softly.

"So you ended up asking your brother for help."

"He was the only one with any money because he took over everything from my father, who apparently had bled all the packs dry. I found out he took any cash they had, and Juneau had that. So my education was paid for by my father and brother using money they stole from the various packs and goodness knows where else," he said, guilt clear in his voice. "It seems that everything I thought I'd built in my life is tainted by my father."

"Then the best thing to do is to put the education we both have to work for the pack. I know that's what I need to do. The pack here supported me through my education, and I need to repay them somehow." Too bad he'd spent the last year ignorantly avoiding them because he thought he didn't fit in any longer. "I know I have plenty of debts to repay myself."

Fredrik nodded. "How about we get dressed and then figure out how we can help out around here? If I'm going to stay, I need to make myself useful. But first we should clean up, and I'm going to need some of those clothes you promised." Fredrik rolled on top of him, and Christopher hugged him, letting his hands roam down Fredrik's back and over his firm butt.

"I think clothes are overrated, especially on you."

"They are?"

"Oh yes. I think I'll keep you here, naked, for a while. I like being naked with you." He guided Fredrik's lips to his and kissed him with heat that quickly built to a blaze.

HE AND Fredrik stayed where they were for another hour, but then his stomach decided to make its wants known. Christopher dressed and went to the pack house, where he got some clothes for Fredrik.

"What did you two decide?" Mikael asked, cornering him in the kitchen as Christopher was about to leave.

"He's going to stay for a little while, and I intend to see to it that he has the time of his life." He smiled. "I was also thinking that maybe you and I could go over the pack's business."

Mikael narrowed his eyes in suspicion. "Why?"

"I don't want the keys to the pack accounts or anything. But I took a lot of business classes, and maybe I can help the pack get the most for its money. I'm assuming that you generate most of the money for the pack with your artwork."

"Yes. Not all, but a good portion."

"Then maybe there are things we can do to generate a little extra money."

"We've always been relatively self-sufficient. You know that."

"Yes. But more and more, there are things we need that we can't make or grow ourselves. So I was thinking maybe we could talk about how we can do more as a pack."

Mikael looked at him with that piercing gaze of his. "That could be a good idea. Let's talk about it. Get your ideas together, and Denton and I will be happy to listen." His gaze softened and eventually Mikael smiled. "It's good to have you back." He took his coffee, and Christopher heard the stairs creak as Mikael bounded upstairs.

"Be sure to close the windows," Christopher said.

Bastard.

Christopher smiled and went outside. He felt better than he had in quite a while. It was time he made an effort to rejoin his family. Yeah, he wasn't sure what he was going to do, but at least he had the beginnings of a plan. Now he needed to find Fredrik a role in the pack and make him happy so he'd stay, and he only had a few days.

Christopher hurried out the back to the guest cabin. The clothes would be big on Fredrik, but it was better than him wearing the same things over and over again. He stepped inside and heard the sound of water. Instantly an image of his mate, naked and wet, flashed in his head. He hurried through the cabin, set the clothes on the bed, and pushed open the bathroom door.

Yum. The scent of his mate, water, and herbal soap combined into a delicious airborne enticement. Christopher stripped and then pushed back the rear of the curtain, climbed in, and pressed his chest to his mate's back. "I bet this has never happened to you before." Christopher lightly kissed and then licked Fredrik's shoulder. Damn, his mate tasted good.

"You mean being snuck up on by a wolf in the shower?" Fredrik dramatically pretended to think. "I don't think so. I've been snuck up on by many wolves in my time, but none in the shower. Unless you count the times when I was a cub and my brothers decided to gang up on me with their towels."

"No. I don't mean that at all." Christopher tensed. "You do realize that if I ever meet any of these brothers, I'm going to have to kill them." He could feel his wolf rising and breathed normally to calm his racing heart and settle his wolf.

"We went to the swimming hole, and when we got out, Juneau instigated a towel fight, and suddenly they all turned on me. I had black and blue marks all over me for days. After that, I never went swimming again."

"Never?" Christopher asked.

"Not even to the pool when I was in college."

Christopher reached for the shampoo and put a dab on his palm. He lathered and then washed his mate's hair. It was so soft. He wanted to bury his fingers in it forever. He massaged Fredrik's scalp and then let him rinse.

He held Fredrik to him, his throbbing cock pressed to Fredrik's buttcheeks. Damn, he wanted to be inside his mate, to feel his body grip him. Christopher quivered with anticipatory energy. His wolf wanted the same thing, and when Fredrik wriggled his tight little butt, Christopher got all the go-ahead he needed. Fredrik leaned back against him, and Christopher grabbed the soap and slicked his hands to wash his mate. This was his first real opportunity to explore him, and Christopher took advantage. He stroked Fredrik's chest. It wasn't defined, but toned and nice. He spent a lot of time rubbing Fredrik's belly and sides, the vulnerable areas, and it only added more heat when Fredrik lifted his hands over his head, stretching and giving Christopher more access.

Christopher pressed them both forward, the water pouring over them, washing away the last vestiges of soap and shampoo.

Fredrik turned off the water, but neither of them moved. Slowly, the cooler air from outside the shower invaded their space. Their combined warmth kept it at bay for a while, but eventually Fredrik shivered, and Christopher pulled away before pushing open the curtain and grabbing two towels from the bars.

They dried themselves quickly, the energy between them ramping up.

A sharp knock on the outside door interrupted them. "Christopher, I could use your help." He recognized Jerry's voice.

"It looks like we just found a way to help out," Christopher said, trying not to sound disappointed. "We'll be right out," he added more loudly, for Jerry's benefit. Christopher lightly swatted Fredrik's bare butt and then rubbed it, pressing them together once again. "Later on, you'll be all mine, and I promise you I'll make you forget everything, including your name." Fredrik quivered a little, and Christopher captured his lips in a deep kiss that made his head swim. He had to stop or he was going to take Fredrik right now.

"Okay," Fredrik said, pulling back. "We have work to do." He seemed excited, so Christopher opened the bathroom door and began dressing. He watched Fredrik as he pulled on the clean clothes and discovered two important things. First, he loved Fredrik wearing his clothes; it only reinforced to him as well as his wolf that Fredrik was his. Second, it brought home just how much smaller Fredrik was than him. They would need to get Fredrik some pants that fit. Fredrik could still wear his shirts. Hell, Christopher really liked that idea.

"I'm ready," Fredrik said excitedly, looking down at himself. "Well, mostly ready. If I didn't have the belt, the pants would end up around my ankles." He sat on the edge of the bed and rolled up the pant legs so he wouldn't trip as he walked. "Okay, let's go and see what we can help with."

Christopher followed Fredrik out of the cabin and to where Jerry was building another house close to the woods. This one was farther away from the main compound than the others. "What can we do to help?" Christopher asked as he looked up at the partially completed structure. The basic frame had been put together and some of the log walls had been raised.

Jerry turned to both of them. "The walls are getting just high enough that we need more hands to raise the logs." Jerry's gaze narrowed on Fredrik. "I don't think we've met."

"This is my mate, Fredrik," Christopher said, and Jerry's serious expression turned to a wide grin.

"Well, that's good news. Finding a mate is always cause for celebration." Jerry shifted his gaze to each of them in turn and then looked down at the rough-hewn table that held his drawings and plans. "Alpha said you were looking for things to do to help out, and I could sure use two more sets of hands right now. I really want to get the outside shell of the house done so we can shift to inside work and have it ready before winter."

"Who is the cabin for?" Christopher asked.

Jerry blinked twice. "Why, you, of course." He acted surprised that Christopher didn't know.

"Why me?"

"Alpha said he was going to need a place for you to live other than in the pack house. So we started building this a month ago." Jerry shrugged. "Don't ask me why or how. Alpha told me what he wanted, and we began work."

Christopher shared a confused look with Fredrik.

"What do you want us to do?" Fredrik asked, as though what Jerry had just said was nothing out of the ordinary. "Alphas have ways of knowing things," he said to Christopher. "My father always seemed to, so I learned not to question it." He turned to Jerry. "I haven't done much of this kind of work, but I can use a hammer and basic tools."

"I'm going to have you fetch and haul, if that's okay. There are always things that everyone needs. Christopher, we have a number of logs ready to be added, so your help would be appreciated there. Once we have these logs in place and fully attached, we can start raising the roof."

"Okay," Fredrik said with a huge grin. "I'm ready. Where should I start?"

A couple of the wolves who were working to secure the last logs that had been raised turned away and suddenly seemed very busy. Christopher stifled a growl.

"You can work with me." Alpha Denton stepped from around the building and caught the eye of the two wolves, whose bravado faded quickly. "I'm putting together the window casings, and an extra set of hands to steady and hold would be great."

"Yes, Alpha," Fredrik said as his tension and nerves increased. Christopher wondered what that was all about.

"Call me Denton, or Alpha Denton, if that's more comfortable for you."

Fredrik nodded and walked around to the other side of the building.

Christopher watched him go and wondered what was wrong. He was missing something and wasn't sure what the hell it could be.

"Everyone knows who he is and who his father was," Jerry said once Fredrik was gone. "There are those who aren't comfortable around him because of that. I think maybe your mate senses that."

"Do you think Alpha Denton is one of them?" Christopher asked. He doubted it but was hoping for confirmation.

"No, I don't. Otherwise he wouldn't have specifically asked for them to work together. Maybe your mate is just picking up on some general unease? It will pass soon enough."

Christopher hoped so. He wanted his mate to be welcome here, not to feel like an outsider, or worse, as someone to be regarded with suspicion. He'd foolishly thought that once he'd found his mate, everything was going to be okay. Instead, there was a lot to do and only a short time to make Fredrik feel truly welcome.

CHAPTER 3

FREDRIK EXPECTED there to be some resentment and ill feelings from the pack. He had no illusions about his father and what he'd done. So he fully expected everything from cold shoulders to outright hostility. What he hadn't expected was Alpha Denton to come to his rescue, or for him to feel so unsettled by the snubs.

"Don't worry," Denton said. "This pack has been through a lot, but they're good people, and they'll understand soon enough that you aren't your father." He showed Fredrik what to hold and carefully attached the pieces.

"I'm surprised you're talking to me." Fredrik let go and took hold of the next corner while Denton got ready. "I know you and your pack took the brunt of my father's wrath."

Denton put down his tools. "You aren't your father, and you are not responsible for his actions. You proved yourself to be a very different person than he is simply because you put yourself in danger for someone else. Anton would never have done that. So let that notion go. Others will see the same thing in time."

Fredrik wanted to believe him.

Denton picked up his tools again and went back to work. They continued for a while, building the casings and then checking them against the openings before finalizing them and adding the glass. It was cool to be working with his hands and to be part of a pack project.

It was near lunchtime and they were finishing up the first window installation when a chill raced up Fredrik's spine. He knew he was being watched. He looked around. The others were all at their tasks, so he focused his attention on the trees nearby. "Someone is out there." He knew deep down it was someone his brother had sent to find him. Fredrik stepped closer to the uncompleted building, wishing he could become part of the wood and disappear. "I can feel them."

"How?" Denton asked as he turned his attention to the woods. He motioned to the others and told one of the nearby men to get Mikael right away.

"I don't know. I can just feel them out there. They're looking for me." Movement caught his eye, and Fredrik pointed.

"I see them," Denton said. "They're traveling fast." He took off, and other wolves followed.

Fredrik began pulling off his clothes, but Christopher stopped him.

"Go into the pack house and stay there. If it's your brother, you'll be safer there." Christopher was already nearly naked and getting ready to shift. "Please."

Fredrik hurried across the compound and stood on the deck of the pack house as he watched the wolves with Christopher shift and race off into the trees. Then he opened the door as other pack members hurried toward him. Mothers raced by with pups in their arms. Fredrik took a little boy from a pregnant woman and helped her inside.

"Oh, thank you," she said.

"Mama," the little pup cried and began to squirm.

"It's okay, Vadi. I'm right here."

Fredrik got a stool for her, and she sat. He handed her Vadi, who turned in her lap to watch. "I'm Fredrik," he said to the little one with a smile.

"This is Vadim, and I'm Carol. You're working with my mate on the new cabin."

"You're Jerry's wife," Fredrik said, putting things together. He had a lot of names to remember.

"Yes," she said. "I'm okay now. Thank you."

Karl, the large beta, came in and looked around. He seemed to be checking that everyone was accounted for.

"Is this like when Alpha Mikael went after Anton?"

"No, Misha," a woman who Fredrik assumed was the pup's mother answered. "They're only checking to make sure we're all safe. I'm sure they'll be back soon." She patted him on the head, and Alexi joined her, both boys pressed tightly to either side, clutching her hands. "I'm Anna, and I think you know the boys," she said.

"We shared a car ride yesterday." He knelt down, and the boys stood still, fear radiating from both of them. "I'm sure Alpha Mikael and Alpha Denton are going to be okay." He sent a silent wish out to the powers that be for Christopher to be okay as well. He stood and nodded to Anna before following Karl outside.

"They won't be gone long. Whoever was out there was in a hurry to get away," Karl said.

"I think it might be someone my brother sent to try to find me," Fredrik explained. "I'm sorry I'm bringing this down on all of you." He knew he should never have agreed to stay and distance was the only solution that would keep everyone safe.

"We don't know anything yet. It could be a rogue or someone interested in the pack. We've had a few wolves wander onto pack land in the last couple of years. They were looking for shelter and security after their old pack fell apart," Karl explained.

Fredrik was grateful he didn't specify that it was his father's doing, but Fredrik knew it nonetheless. Much of the hurt, pain, and turmoil the packs in this part of the country were going through was the fault of his family.

A cry went up in the forest. It wasn't threatening or fearful, so he interpreted it as saying everyone was all right.

Karl listened and then nodded. He returned it without shifting, sending a call over the trees. "We need to wait here and keep everyone inside," Karl said.

"Do you know what's going on?" Cries and calls had various meanings, especially within a pack. It was a way of communicating. Some cries, like grief and joy, were fairly universal, but others were more specific and developed within the pack structure itself. This one seemed to have meaning, but Fredrik couldn't decipher it.

·"Everyone is okay, and I think they're on their way back. But we need to be cautious." Karl was as vigilant as anyone Fredrik had ever seen. Within a few minutes, wolves began to emerge from the trees, followed by a few who had shifted to human form. They dressed quickly and stood at the ready until Mikael and Denton stepped out of the woods with Christopher and then a huge wolf bringing up the rear, holding on to the arm of a strange wolf. "That's Catherine in the back."

"Damn, she's scary as hell."

"There's a reason she's the enforcer. With her children and pack, she's kind, but cross her or the pack and she's the devil incarnate. I still have a few scars from when we were kids."

Fredrik nodded as his gaze followed Christopher. Damn, his mate was stunning—strong, but not huge, trim and neat, with a butt that could crack walnuts and…. His cock decided it really liked what he was seeing, and he was happy his pants were bulky, even if others could smell his arousal. There seemed to be enough in the air at the moment as other mates became aroused.

The wolves all shifted and dressed. Finally, Denton jogged up toward the deck and motioned for them to come down. He met them at the base of the steps and stayed with Fredrik as they came forward.

"Stephan?" Fredrik asked as he approached. "What are you doing here?"

"Your brother sent me to find you. He said you'd taken off and that you'd killed Dimitri and taken one of his prizes when you left."

Fredrik nodded. "I did all that, and I would have killed Juneau as well. But why would you come? You aren't like him. Is he forcing you?"

Stephan shook his head. "I volunteered. When you got away, I thought I'd try to do the same. My mother is gone, so it's just me now." Stephan dropped to his knees and stared down at the ground. "I always liked you and hoped that if I found you again…."

Christopher growled and stepped between them. "He's my mate, and you'd better get any ideas you might have out of your mind now."

Stephan nodded and looked dejected. "You have a mate?·Like, a real mate?"

"Yes. And you're really pissing him off," Fredrik said.

"I'd never come between mates," Stephan said, shaking slightly.

"Stephan was never one of Juneau's inner circle," Fredrik said. "I'm not sure why he'd even send him unless he was convinced he had Stephan completely intimidated." Fredrik turned back to Stephan even as he put his hand on Christopher's shoulder to calm him down.

"I think you need to tell all of us why you're here," Mikael said. "You were found skulking around on pack land uninvited, and you're a known associate of this pack's sworn enemy." He leaned forward. "We would be within our rights to have you ripped apart and dumped in the woods for the carrion." He pulled Stephan to his feet and marched him the short distance to the edge of the compound. Then he pushed him back to the ground.

"Is it safe for the others?" Karl asked.

"Yes. They can go back to what they were doing. But everyone needs to be on the lookout. Remind them what happened the last time a member of this man's family had their sights on this pack," Mikael answered.

"I will," Karl said and hurried away.

Fredrik stood off to the side, watching Stephan and doing his best to stay out of the way.

"What do you know about this guy?" Christopher asked.

"He's my half brother and was never one of the pack members in Juneau's favor, if that's what you're asking. He's a lot like me. He tried to stay out of my father's way as much as possible. I guess I'm surprised he didn't return to one of the reforming packs the way most of the wolves did."

"My mother," Stephan answered. "She was in love with the bastard. I don't know why, but she was, and she refused to leave even after he was killed. She said that was her home and she wasn't leaving. I couldn't leave her alone with them, so I stayed to try to take care of her."

"Is this true?" Mikael asked, looking at Fredrik.

"It fits with what I know. Though she'd have to be crazy to love Anton. But then maybe that was what they had in common, she loved Anton and so did my father. The only person he ever loved was himself," Fredrik spat.

"So why are you here?" Mikael asked, looking at Stephen.

"Juneau said Fredrik had probably brought the girl back here. He said I was to find out and then return and tell him. From there he said he'd know what to do. None of the others wanted to come because they're all afraid of the alphas here. I figured I didn't have much to lose and thought that if I got here, I could maybe see if I could join the pack. There's nothing for me back there."

"Then why didn't you just walk up to the house and knock on the door?" Mikael said. "If that was what you wanted to do, there was no need to sneak up on us. But you did, so your story doesn't hold water with me."

"I had to. I've heard about this pack. Everyone is talking about it. I had to see if it was for real. I mean, everything is a mess out there, and this pack is thriving and everyone is happy. That seemed like too much to believe. So I stayed in the trees and watched. The thing is, even Fredrik seems happy, and he's only been here… what, a day?"

Mikael knelt down next to Stephan. "I don't believe you, but I don't smell any lies or deception on you either. So here's what we're going to do. You are going to tell Denton and me everything you know about Juneau, including how many people are loyal to him and what his plans are. If you lie, we'll dump you off our land and you can fend for yourself or go back to Juneau and hope he's feeling forgiving."

"And if I help you?"

Mikael glanced at Christopher. "Then we'll discuss the possibility of pack membership. But you need to be honest in all things."

"I will," Stephan said.

"All right. Come with us." Mikael helped Stephan up, and he and Alpha Denton escorted him away to talk.

Fredrik watched, wondering what he should do.

"What do you think about this guy?" Christopher asked once they were alone.

"He was one of the few people who was nice to me. I really don't think he's a threat to anyone." Fredrik wrung his hands a few times. "What I don't understand is what my brother is up to. He had to know that Stephan wanted to get away, so why would he send him?"

"Is your brother thinking clearly? Or maybe he doesn't have that many people loyal to him and he's getting desperate."

Fredrik shook his head. "It's more likely he didn't send Stephan alone." He turned toward the trees. "Did you scent anyone else out there?"

"No."

"Well, think about it. Juneau probably knows that Stephan and I were friends of a sort, so he sent him knowing we might let down our guard. He gets Stephan to find me and has other men waiting to either take me or cause havoc here. And it's working. Mikael has pulled all the wolves from the trees, and everyone is going back to their tasks as though nothing has happened. As if the real danger is over."

"I believe you," Christopher said. He hurried across the compound to Catherine.

Fredrik saw him talking to her, and then they both stripped, shifted, and raced into the trees. Fredrik remained vigilant, watching the trees for movement. The pack as a whole was still in danger; he could feel it. He'd sensed someone in the trees, and it wasn't Stephan. It had been someone darker and blacker. Someone much closer to his father.

While Mikael and Denton spoke with Stephan, Jerry and the others went back to work on the cabin. Fredrik wished he could tell them all to go inside and be safe for now, but he wasn't convinced anyone would believe him.

A cry went up from the trees, this one clear to all: distress. It sent a chill racing up Fredrik's spine. His mate was out there, and he'd only just found him. A howl pierced the late morning. Denton and Mikael leaped, shifting once again. Fredrik stripped as well and shifted as fast as he could before tearing off into the trees behind them. There was no way in hell he was going to stay behind with his mate out there in possible danger.

The trees were unfamiliar, but he was able to dash around them, easily following the scent trail. He slowed as Christopher's scent grew stronger, mixed with the iron scent of blood. Something was very wrong. He grew more worried, and he was cautious as he approached what appeared to be a light spot in the trees.

Christopher was still in wolf form, standing in the tall grass. Fredrik hurried over and began sniffing and looking him over. There was blood on his coat, and Fredrik licked him, determining it wasn't his.

"What happened?" Denton asked as he shifted, with Mikael right behind him.

"Hunters," Catherine answered once she shifted. Christopher did the same, and Fredrik followed suit, noticing that Christopher immediately stepped between him and the others. "Christopher took this one down as he was about to take a shot." Catherine pointed to the body on the ground. "Then we ran the others off. But I think they have a camp nearby. They are too far from home not to have some base of operation."

"I say we track them and take them out," Christopher said.

Mikael and Denton looked at each other and seemed to be communicating. Denton nodded and then nodded again a few seconds later. "Their scent isn't going anywhere on a sunny day like this. I want to go back to the compound and get it buttoned down. Then we'll get a party together to hunt these guys and see if we can't figure out what they know and where they came from."

"Alpha," Fredrik said. "I don't think this is a coincidence."

"What?"

"I overheard a conversation a few weeks ago. I didn't know what it meant then, but I think I do now. Juneau was talking to Yuri, and he told him that he had arranged some outside support for his cause. What if this was that support?"

"A wolf working with hunters?" Mikael asked.

"An unholy alliance if I ever heard one," Catherine muttered.

"Yeah. But think about it. Juneau uses the hunters to weaken or take out his enemies, and then he can take over everything, just like my father did."

"Son of a bitch," Mikael said. "All right. If what Fredrik says is true, then we'll need to be extra careful. I want these hunters eliminated, but I don't want any of our family hurt. So we'll develop a solid plan before we do anything."

"We need to find them," Catherine said. "I volunteer."

Fredrik looked at the others. He'd been afraid that Christopher would want to go.

"All right," Mikael said. "But be back in an hour. No longer."

Catherine nodded, shifted back into wolf form, and raced off into the trees.

"Did you search him?" Mikael asked, pointing to the bloody mess that had once been a man.

Fredrik felt no remorse. That man had put his mate in danger; that was all Fredrik needed to know. He bent and began going through the pockets. There wasn't much. He found a wallet in the guy's back pocket, but there was no ID in it, just a few dollars. Fredrik dropped everything and left it with him. "There's nothing else."

"Then let's go back to the compound. We need to plan and be ready to move out as soon as Catherine returns."

FREDRIK WAITED with the others. The hour the alpha had given Catherine was nearly up and all the men were jittery. Fredrik had hoped Christopher would be asked to stay behind, but Jerry and Catherine's husband, Stan, were going to take charge of the compound and keep everyone inside and safe. The others were going to eliminate the hunters.

Finally Catherine's gray-and-black wolf stepped from the trees, and she shifted. Stan had been waiting anxiously with a robe, and he slid it over her shoulders. Catherine was breathing hard as she approached the group and addressed Mikael directly. "Their camp is outside our territory to the northwest. They must have come in on one of the old park roads. There are eight of them, and they seem on edge. I have to say that these men don't seem like the kind to scare easily. My guess is that they started out as survivalists. They expected the end of the world, and when it didn't happen, they turned their attention to other things."

"What are their weapons?"

"I saw one assault rifle and an assortment of other guns. They're armed to the teeth."

"So what do we do?" Fredrik asked.

Mikael grinned. "We instill a little terror and make them wish they'd never left home." He looked up toward the sky. "It's afternoon. We all need to eat well and get some rest. We'll meet in the pack cave in two hours. We're going to need the Mother's support for this. We'll leave an hour before sunset and get into position as it gets dark. Then we'll see if we can't give them all a very sleepless night."

Everyone in the group nodded.

"What about Stephan?" Christopher asked.

"Denton and I need to have a little talk with him and see if he has any more he can tell us. He's scared half out of his wits of Fredrik's brother, so I'm hoping there's no deep loyalty there."

"Would you really let him join the pack?" Fredrik asked quietly.

"If he proved himself, I would. He's related to you, isn't he?"

Fredrik nodded.

"I thought so." Mikael's gaze bore deeply into him, and Fredrik wondered what he was looking for. "Everyone get some food and rest. It's going to be a long night."

Christopher's mother had been cooking up a storm, so they all sat around the table in the main house. She served a meal fit for a holiday feast. It was amazing, and Fredrik thanked her once he got up from the table. He was stuffed to the gills, and all he wanted was a nap. Christopher seemed to have the same idea because he followed him out to the guest cabin. As soon as the door closed behind them,

Fredrik's lethargy disappeared as Christopher pulled him into his arms, kissed him with enough heat that Fredrik thought he might burst into flames, and began tugging off their clothes.

They ended up leaving a trail of fabric between the door and the bed before tumbling down onto the mattress. God, it felt good to be in Christopher's strong arms. He laughed and watched as Christopher crawled up him, his gaze almost feral as it locked onto his. The intensity of his mate's gaze took his breath away, and for a second, he tried to think if anyone else had ever looked at him like that. He came up blank. It was as if he were the center of the world at that moment, and damn if he didn't love that feeling.

"I'm going to make you scream for me," Christopher whispered.

"You are?" Fredrik's mouth went Sahara dry.

"Oh yeah. I'm going to suck you just enough so you're shaking, and then I think I'll eat you out, turn you to mush before sliding inside your tight little ass." Christopher locked their gazes, and Fredrik swallowed to try to answer, but all he managed was a small nod. "I want you more than I've wanted anyone." Christopher took his lips as though he were a pirate ship to be plundered, and Fredrik adored it and burned with each touch.

When Christopher broke the kiss, Fredrik whimpered like a pup and then groaned. Christopher licked and sucked at his neck, harder and more intensely by the second. "You're mine," he whispered.

"Are you marking me?"

"For now." Christopher moved to the other side, and Fredrik stretched his neck to give him access to continue his erotic torture.

Fredrik gripped the bedding in his fists, his hands burning as his wolf tried to make an appearance. He wanted to stay human and enjoy this, but it took all his willpower to keep his wolf from bursting out.

Christopher licked down his chest and belly, leaving a trail of small nips that set him on fire.

"How did you know what I liked?"

"I'm your mate. If you were fragile and gentle, you wouldn't have been for me. I like my sex athletic and extremely tactile." Christopher proved it by sliding his lips down Fredrik's cock, sending a zing of amazing energy up his back, and it bloomed into warmth that spread through the rest of his body.

"Chris...." Fredrik groaned as Christopher took all of him inside sweet wet heat.

"Did I lie?" Christopher asked him after letting his cock slip from his mouth.

Fredrik's answer came out as a whimper, and Christopher sucked him again, harder and faster. Within seconds, his overactive libido had him on edge. He hadn't felt he was going to come that fast since he was a teenager. "This mate thing is amazing," Fredrik moaned.

"You haven't seen anything yet." Christopher lifted Fredrik's legs and buried his lips and tongue between his cheeks.

Fucking hell, no one had ever done that before, and he shook harder than a leaf in a gale.

"Oh my gosh...." Fredrik gasped as his wolf got closer to the surface.

"Calm your wolf. This is for both of you, but I need you in charge," Christopher said, and Fredrik swallowed and forced his wolf back from the surface.

He had never had trouble controlling his shift before, but his wolf was desperate to be around his mate. The two of them needed to run together, but later... much later. Fredrik gasped for breath as Christopher took him to ecstasy in a way he had never dreamed. More than once Fredrik reached for his cock as the need to come grew greater, but Christopher batted his hand away each time, driving him wild and making him wait.

"Are you ready for me?" Christopher asked.

"I don't have anything...."

Christopher leaped off the bed and grabbed his pants. He rummaged in his pockets and then dropped them back to the floor. He ripped open the sachet and spread some of the slick on Fredrik's opening. Christopher then coated his cock and got back into position. "This isn't going to be gentle." Sweat had broken out on Christopher's forehead, and he was shaking almost as badly as Fredrik.

"Yes," Fredrik cried when Christopher pressed forward and his body opened to him. The stretch whooshed the breath from his lungs, and he began to sweat like crazy as Christopher entered him. Fredrik gasped and gritted his teeth. Christopher pushed deeper, filling him completely. "A second," Fredrik moaned, and Christopher stilled briefly and then pressed home.

"God, you're perfect," Christopher groaned. He leaned forward and kissed him hard, pulsing his hips in just the right way so Fredrik saw stars.

His head spun, and he held Christopher tight so he wouldn't fly to pieces. Being with Christopher was so intense. "You were right," Fredrik hummed as Christopher straightened slightly and moved inside him.

"Is this exactly what you needed?"

"Yes."

"Me too," Christopher whispered. "It's what's been missing from my life. You…. I was unhappy because I didn't think I fit anywhere."

"You fit with me." Fredrik groaned and his eyes rolled as a wave of passion crashed over him. It was damn near too much. His wolf was just as happy, and Fredrik pressed back against Christopher, moving with him in a dance that brought them closer to the pinnacle of matehood with each movement. "I have to come. I need it."

"Then do it. Come for me, right now." Christopher drove into him, and Fredrik went wild. He wanted to please his mate so much that he was instantly overcome by a shaking desire that washed over him. He lost control of his own body, instinct taking over, and he came blindingly hard, yelling at the top of his lungs, with Christopher following right behind him.

Fredrik lay still, heart beating in his ears. He heard Christopher's heart and breathing, felt him holding him as they lay together after having their minds blown. Fredrik loved Christopher's weight on him, and a light breeze cooled their skin.

The breeze. Fredrik realized the windows were open, and that meant half the pack had most likely heard them. He felt his cheeks color. "I think we had an audience," he whispered.

"You'll get used to it. With dozens of wolf ears around, there is very little that's private." As if to emphasize his point, cries carried in through the window from around the compound.

Fredrik rolled onto his side and then buried his face in a pillow.

"Is something wrong?" Christopher asked, and Fredrik lifted his face. Tears streamed down his cheeks, and he tried to keep from laughing. Christopher chuckled and then pulled him close.

"I can't help myself."

"We're all wolves, and some of us are going into battle. So that means that we spend time with our mates, making sure they know how we feel. It gives us strength. Denton is with Mikael right now, I'm sure of it, just like all the others warriors are with their mates. I asked my dad why it was like that, and he said being with your mate before battle or a challenge was like taking them with you. It allowed you to carry their strength and love along with you. I thought he was being sentimental until now."

"I think I agree with him." Fredrik rubbed Christopher's back, closing his eyes and letting sleep and contentment wash over him. They had a little while before they were to gather to leave, so they might as well rest.

Of course, Fredrik was too keyed up to actually do much more than lie there. Even after mind-blowing sex, he was still wound too tight. He kept thinking all of this excitement wouldn't be happening if he'd simply continued on after bringing Jane back. He wouldn't be putting his mate and his mate's pack in danger. Of course, he wouldn't have known any of that, because coming back to the compound with Mikael had allowed him to meet Christopher. He wished he knew why things worked like this.

There is always the good with the bad. Everything must remain in balance.

Fredrik sat straight up. "What was that? Did you say something?"

"No. What did you hear?"

Fredrik shook his head. He must have been hearing things. Either that or his wolf hearing had tuned in to a conversation across the compound. "It was nothing." Fredrik continued listening, but he didn't hear the voice again.

"Just relax. We have an hour before we need to get up and join the others for the trip to the cave."

"What cave? Like the one you were living in?"

"Yes and no. This cave is one of the ones where we lived and hid to be safe when the wolves had been hunted almost to extinction. It was a safe place, and it's close to the Mother. Whenever there are important pack decisions to be made or if we need to make sure we're united or to pray for the Mother's blessing, we go there. It's now a sacred place for the pack." Christopher tightened his hold. "Just close your eyes. Everything will be made clear for you in time. It's easier to show you and let you feel it than it is to try to describe the feeling of being in the cave."

"Okay." Fredrik closed his eyes and tried to relax. Growing up, he'd never been taught to pray or worship any particular deity. His father wanted everyone to spend their time and effort taking care of him and seeing to what he wanted.

That's because your father was not of the light. But now you have the chance to grow and flourish without his interference.

"Did you hear that?"

Of course he didn't. I'm speaking to you. A chuckle followed and then silence.

Fredrik was going crazy. That was the only explanation. He was hearing voices now and probably needed to have his head examined. Was there such a thing as a shifter psychologist? If there was, he needed to make an appointment right away. His heart rate increased, and he continued listening. Soon the only sounds he heard were Christopher's gentle snores. Great. Everyone was going to be rested and he was going to slow them down.

"Just go to sleep," Christopher murmured.

Fredrik closed his eyes, and the next thing he knew, he jerked awake when Christopher got up and began dressing. "Is it time to go?"

"Yeah. I can hear the others gathering outside."

Fredrik got up and began pulling on his clothes.

"We'll be traveling as wolves most of the time, so keep your clothing to a minimum—less to remove and take care of."

Great. Fredrik dressed, and then he and Christopher joined the others in the compound. He felt better rested than he thought he would.

Mikael seemed to take note of who was present and motioned for them to follow him. No one spoke, so Fredrik kept quiet as well. The party wound along down a path that led into a sloping canyon and down to a creek bed. Christopher held his hand as they walked, but remained quiet like the others. Eventually they all stopped. Mikael pulled the vegetation away from the cave entrance, then undressed and shifted, entering as a wolf. The others did the same, so Fredrik followed suit.

The cave entrance was small, and he had to duck to get through. He understood why this would be the perfect place to hide during the decades that their kind had scraped by to survive. He'd heard a few stories over the years, but passing on oral history had never been high on his father's priority list.

Once he'd passed through the low entrance, he saw the cave opened into a large room. He could see a small group of shifters subsisting here. It was remote, and it wasn't likely that anyone would stumble on the cave. Candles had been lit, and they added an air of mystery as the light danced off the stone ceiling. Fredrik shifted, and Christopher handed him a white robe. He put it on the way the others had and continued looking around. A small raised area seemed to act as a speaking platform. Mikael and Denton stood there together.

"We are here to ask the Mother for her blessing as we try to protect ourselves. Contrary to the image humans have of us from their movies and books, we are not a violent people. We live in packs so we can care for each other. We kill to protect ourselves."

The others nodded slowly.

"However, we are being hunted, and if we are to be safe, we must attack."

Taking life is always the last resort for the children of the light.

Fredrik looked around, but no one else seemed to have heard anything, and they continued to listen to Mikael. He definitely was going out of his mind.

No, you aren't.

"Who are you?" Fredrik murmured, the words carried on his breath they were said so softly. He knew Christopher heard him, but the others didn't seem to.

Who do you think I am?

"A voice in my head."

A chuckle followed. *I am that. But so much more. I am the one you are here to discover. You wonder if I really exist, but I do. Your mother was a child of the light, one of my children. She believed she could bring light to the darkness.*

"I don't understand."

You are one of my people, if you choose to be. There is darkness in you. I can feel it, and you know it's there too. It comes from your father. There will be a battle.

"Between Juneau and this pack?"

The battle will be fought for your heart and soul.

"I don't understand."

You will, eventually. He heard another chuckle, though this time it seemed farther away. Mikael was still talking. *I think I need to teach your alpha that less is sometimes more.* The voice was mirthful, and suddenly a wind filled the air, blowing the flames of the candles and lightly swirling around each of them.

Fredrik closed his eyes, and for a second, he felt his mother's hands on him, embracing him the way she used to when things got too hard and too mean at home. She'd comfort him, and he felt that same comfort now.

"Thank you," Mikael said loudly. "Your blessing is appreciated." The breeze trailed off, and the air became still once again. "Her blessing does not ensure victory. That is up to us. These hunters may work together, but they are not a pack, and they are not defending their home. Each of you say what you need to, and then we'll head back to make final preparations." Mikael held Denton's hand in his.

"We are Old Faithful," Denton said. "We chose that name not only because of the gift of water the Mother bestows on us and our home, but because it describes who we are and how we behave to each other. We are true and honest, but strong and enduring. We will protect what is ours and those we love."

Fredrik expected a yell or a show of aggression and enthusiasm—they certainly would have been yelling if his father had been speaking. He was ready to punch the air and shout, but when he looked around, all he saw was serious determination on each and every face. Once the alphas were done speaking, the wolves took off their robes, folded them and put them away, shifted, and then left the cave. Fredrik followed Christopher and did what he did.

Once back out in the open air, they gathered into a group, waiting for the alphas, who came out last. Then they all turned their heads upward, crying out, sending their voices to the sky. After a few seconds, replies were heard, adult voices mixed with the yips and cries of pups. What Christopher had said was right: they were all going into battle, as a pack, and even those who stayed behind were with them in spirit.

When the cries died away on the wind, Mikael led them back to the compound at a run.

Some of the pack chose to remain in wolf form while others dressed in dark clothes and retrieved weapons. Catherine was formidable as a wolf, but dressed in full commando gear, she'd give Rambo a run for his money. That woman was fierce, without a doubt.

"We need to be silent," she said. "It will be dark soon enough, but if we keep up a fast pace, we can reach them as they're hunkering down for the night. Let those in wolf form lead the way."

"What's the plan?" Christopher asked.

"Divide and conquer, if we can. Lead one of them away from the others and take him out. It's that simple. Work together. Harass them. The more jittery they become, the more mistakes they will make." Catherine walked over to where Fredrik and Christopher stood together. "You don't have to come. This isn't your fight."

Fredrik looked at Christopher and then back at her. "Yes, I do."

She loomed over him, her expression clearly asking why.

"You have been good to me. All of you have. And this is my fault. These hunters are here because of me. I have to help make this right." He nearly said he'd go into battle with his mate, but he stopped those words cold. Every minute he was with Christopher was right and drew them closer; he could feel it. But he was bringing pain and danger to this pack just by being here. The trouble they were having was because of him, and they didn't deserve any of it.

Catherine seemed to accept his answer. "You two are with me."

Denton and Mikael led the way into the trees, and the rest of the group followed.

There were ten of them in total, but even with his sensitive hearing, Fredrik would never have known it. No one spoke and they all moved nearly silently. Darkness fell quickly in the shade, but his enhanced vision helped him maneuver quickly and easily over the forest floor. After all, it was home to a huge part of himself, and he'd always been comfortable in the woods. There was nothing frightening or scary there, other than them. They were the top-line predator, in either form, and all other creatures got out of their way.

Catherine guided the party, and as she predicted, they arrived near the camp as the last light disappeared from the sky. The hunters were easy to spot with their fire and conversation. They clearly thought they were invincible and no one would dare approach them. Catherine was also correct about their numbers, and they spoke loudly enough that everyone could easily hear them.

68

"They're on edge about their missing man, so that will work in our favor." Catherine only had to whisper and everyone could hear her.

"Denton and I will work around to the other side," Mikael said. "When you hear our cry, I suspect some of them will come after us. See if you can get another group to follow you. When you take them out, do it as silently as possible." Everyone nodded to indicate they had heard. Mikael and Denton stripped and shifted, then disappeared from the group.

Fredrik stared at the group of men through the trees, listening to their conversation.

"I wish Garreth would get back," one of them whined, nervously. "I should never have let you talk me into this."

"You pussy," the man next to him chided, smacking him on the shoulder. "Go feed the dogs if all you can do is whine."

Fredrik knitted his brows together. Catherine hadn't said anything about dogs. He hoped to hell they stayed quiet and didn't raise an alarm too early. He scented the air and crinkled his nose as he got a whiff of men who hadn't bathed in way too long, garbage, and what had to be an open hole they were using as a toilet. All those smells prevented him from scenting much else, which was frustrating.

"I want to get out of here."

"Why? We're here to do what's right and wipe these abominations of nature off the earth." The man speaking was huge, and from the way he looked at the others, he was clearly the leader. In many ways, he reminded Fredrik of his brother, a bully to the core.

A wolf howl split the night, and the men were instantly on alert. A second howl followed from a different direction, and the leader pointed to two men, who grabbed their guns and took off toward the woods.

Catherine howled as well, and Fredrik scented fear above all the other stench. A fourth howl went up, and then Christopher called out from behind him. Catherine howled again, and then, just like they'd hoped, two of the men made their way cautiously in her direction.

"I ain't going out there," one of the men said when the leader indicated he was to go. "You go if you're so fucking anxious to get killed." The leader stepped toward the men menacingly, and the other man pointed his rifle. "I'll shoot you before I go out there."

"This is perfect," Christopher said just before a shot rang through the night, followed by another and then silence. Fredrik listened for a cry or howl, but he heard nothing. He hoped all the pack members were okay.

He grew more and more nervous by the second. Maybe he should have stayed back at the compound. All of this was his fault— every bit of it. Fredrik felt Christopher's breath on his neck.

"I can smell your anxiety," Christopher whispered. "Stop all of it. We'll talk it through later, but for now, stay alert and protect the pack."

"And you," Fredrik added.

Christopher patted his shoulder.

They stayed behind a huge tree that provided shadow and cover. Christopher called again, and Fredrik moved around slowly to another large tree and sent up a call himself. His came out low and extra deep as he threw all his anger and guilt into it.

"We're fucking surrounded by those things. I told you this was a stupid idea. And where are the others? They should be back." The four remaining men stood in the light of the fire, looking at each other, their bravado long gone.

Fredrik turned to Christopher, who motioned for him to go around, he assumed, to where Catherine was. Fredrik made his way, and fucking hell if he didn't step on a twig. It snapped, and almost instantly a shot rang out in his direction. Fredrik fell to the ground and didn't move, taking stock to make sure he wasn't hit.

Other shots rang out from the group, wild and erratic. He looked up in time to see one of the men with an automatic weapon as he strafed the woods with gunfire. Fredrik plastered himself to the ground, hoping like hell the fallen trees gave him cover and the others were safe.

The gunfire died and the last echoes faded away. Fredrik held still, afraid to move until a single cry split the night, low and

70

haunting, weak and short. Filled with pain. Fredrik stayed still, pressed to the ground, wondering if he should help while at the same time scared they'd start shooting again. The cry came again, and still he stayed where he was, hesitating in his internal conflict for self-preservation. "Shit," he whispered under his breath and began pulling off his clothes.

Another shot split the night, zinging above his head. Fredrik's heart raced, and his first instinct was to stay the hell where he was. It was so strong that it nearly forced his naked body back to the ground. He shifted as quickly as he could and listened, but heard nothing.

Fredrik took off away from the camp and then doubled back, closing in on where he'd heard the cry. He knew he was getting close when the pungent scent of blood assaulted him. Shots still rang out occasionally, but they quieted quickly. He continued forward, stepping over a human that had been eviscerated. Fredrik didn't stop to look, following the scent of wolf blood.

He found Catherine lying on the ground in wolf form. He sniffed and quickly found the wound. After looking around for danger and sensing none in the immediate area, he shifted back and located the knife he remembered had been on Catherine's belt. "It's okay. I'm going to try to help," he whispered softly so her wolf could hear.

"What happened?" Christopher asked from behind him.

"It looks like she was shot in that last shooting spree. I heard her cries." Fredrik wished he was in wolf form so he could see better, but then he wouldn't have hands, which he was going to need. "Can you shoot?"

"I haven't in years," Christopher said.

Fredrik picked up one of the weapons and placed it in Christopher's hands. "Well, remember everything you were taught and take those bastards out. They shot your sister, and unless I can get the bullet out, she's going to die."

He turned back to Catherine and used his fingers to find the wound. She was still bleeding, which should have stopped. That meant the bullet had silver in it. He swore under his breath and poked around. Catherine grunted, but he thanked God for the animal-anatomy class

71

he'd taken when he thought he was going to be a veterinarian. She was still alive, but he had to get the bullet out fast.

Fredrik kept his hand steady when Christopher opened fire near him. "I found it," he whispered and used the blade of the knife to lift it out. Then he covered the wound and prayed she hadn't lost so much blood that she wouldn't recover.

Shots rang out, and Fredrik crouched low, still naked and slumped near Catherine to try to keep her warm. He had done what he could do for right now, but he prayed it was enough and he'd gotten there in time. He should have come right away and not cowered on the ground. If he had….

Christopher fired again, and a man cried out. Fredrik heard Christopher mutter about getting the bastard. Shots now rang out from different directions, and Fredrik hoped no one got caught in the crossfire.

"Kill the dogs," a gruff voice yelled, and then the man screamed at the top of his lungs. More shots echoed through the woods, and then all was quiet.

"I think we got them all," Christopher said.

"Be careful when you check," Fredrik said, still curled around Catherine.

Christopher set the rifle down next to him and growled low and menacingly.

"Stop it—I'm trying to keep your sister warm." She moved, and Fredrik stood.

Christopher wrapped him in his arms, then pulled off his own shirt and thrust it into Fredrik's hands. "I don't want my mate flashing everyone."

"For goodness sake, she's hurt and you're jealous." Fredrik was pretty sure he liked that. He put on the shirt and knelt. "Can you shift?" he asked Catherine. "You need to try. It will help you heal."

Catherine's wolf blinked up at him, and then he stepped back as she slowly turned human. As weak as she was, it had to be a difficult ordeal, but once she did, the wound closed. "Thank you."

"I wish I'd gotten here sooner," Fredrik said. "Where are your clothes?"

"Behind that tree. I figured I'd let my wolf have some fun. She desperately wanted to get in the action."

"I think we all underestimated the kind of firepower they had," Christopher said. "We might be able to hunt game, but…."

"It isn't in our nature to hunt people," Catherine said.

Fredrik got her clothes and helped her get dressed.

"Go see if there is anyone left in the camp."

Fredrik and Christopher moved to follow her instructions.

"Is everyone okay?" Mikael asked, his voice carrying.

"Catherine was hit, but she's recovering," Christopher said as they approached the hunters' camp. It was a shambles. Men lay where they fell, the leader groaning slightly, still alive and trying to pull himself away. He was bleeding badly, and Fredrik took the rifle from Christopher and shot him in the head.

"Mercy killing," he explained and handed the rifle back.

Mikael, Denton, and the rest of the party except Catherine stepped into the clearing.

"Where is she?" Mikael asked.

Fredrik pointed in the general direction.

"I'm fine," Catherine called. She sounded weak and angry as hell.

"Search everything and gather any information you can. Take their phones and any computers. We'll see if we can get anything off them before we destroy the things. Bareass Fredrik and Christopher, check the tents."

Christopher growled, and Fredrik smacked him playfully.

"Give it up. Everyone is going to see my ass until I can get back to my clothes."

Christopher pressed right to his back.

"Don't get any ideas, because none of that is happening until we get back to the compound."

Fredrik checked the first tent and found nothing but some clothes and an old sleeping bag and air mattress. He yanked everything out and started sorting through, throwing the trash on the fire. He did find a bag with some clothes that smelled clean and pulled on a pair of the sweatpants he found inside. At least his ass wasn't hanging out any longer. He could change into his own clothes soon enough.

He heard the others checking over the men as he and Christopher went from tent to tent. He found two tablets, a couple of phones, and a laptop that he set aside and Jerry put into a pack for their trip back. He checked the last tent and found nothing more.

"What's that?" Christopher asked, pointing behind the tent. "There's a cage. It could be the dogs they talked about."

"We can't just leave them here," Fredrik said. He hurried over and stopped dead in his tracks about two feet from the small cage. "Those aren't dogs—they're pups." He sniffed again and wanted to scream. "Mikael," he called. "We need you and Denton." Fredrik approached the cage very carefully. He wasn't sure how the pups would react. "I'm not going to hurt you."

The pups weren't very old. They were little more than balls of fluff. When he opened the door, they tried to barrel out past him. Fredrik caught one and Christopher missed the other, but Mikael scooped the little guy up.

"Behave," Mikael said in his alpha voice and then cradled the little one to his chest.

Fredrik followed his example, and his pup calmed the same way Mikael's did.

"What the hell?" Denton asked. "Where did these guys come from and what were hunters doing with them?"

Fredrik shook his head and kept whispering to the pup. "Mikael, can you see if they can shift back?"

"Let's wait to get them back to the compound. It will be easier to travel with them as pups," Catherine suggested from where she sat near the fire. She was pale but definitely looking better, her wolf healing powers kicking in.

"I think we have about all we're going to get here. Everyone dress or shift, and we'll head back in five minutes," Mikael said.

"I'll get your clothes," Christopher said to Fredrik.

74

"Thank you," Fredrik whispered so he didn't upset the pup in his arms. "You're going to be okay. No one is going to hurt you, and we're going to take you where you'll be safe. I promise." He wasn't sure if the pup understood him or was just soothed by his tone.

Christopher returned, and Fredrik gently handed him the pup. He'd been quiet while in Fredrik's arms, but as soon as Christopher reached for him, he bared his teeth, snarling and trying to bite.

"That's not nice. He's trying to help you too," Fredrik said gently, lifting the pup so he could look at him eye to eye. That was when he saw them: the pup's eyes were black, just like his. "Mikael, these pups are related to me."

"How do you know?"

"Black eyes. I have them, and so do my brothers and sisters. All of them. It comes from my father, and as far as I know, my nieces and nephews have the same eyes." Fredrik was really fucking confused about how these pups could have gotten here, and this last piece of information only added to it.

"Let me take him and you get dressed," Mikael said.

Fredrik handed over the little biter, and he seemed to settle now that he was near the other pup. Mikael held one in each arm, and Fredrik pulled off the hunter's clothes and got back into his own. When he reached to take the pup back, they both began to whine.

"I'll take them," Mikael said.

"Don't you need to lead us back?" Fredrik asked respectfully, and Mikael nodded and handed him both pups. They didn't seem to mind being jostled a little as long as they could stay together.

"All right, we're moving out," Mikael commanded. "Jerry, set fire to everything. It's been wet enough lately that it should be all right. We need to leave as little evidence as possible of what happened."

"Yes, Alpha," Jerry said. "We'll be right behind you." He tore down the tents, throwing them onto the fire along with everything else. The flames roared up, consuming everything as he added more and more of what was left of the camp. Some of the others joined in, and within minutes, there was almost nothing left but the remnant fire that was already starting to fade.

Mikael motioned them forward, and the bulk of their group melted into the trees and began the trek back to the compound.

Fredrik talked to the pups almost the entire way. By the end of the trip, his arms were aching, but he wouldn't let either of them get away from him. They needed someone who smelled familiar, and the closest relative they had right now was him.

"Do you have any theories about how they ended up with the hunters?" Denton asked him as they walked.

"I wish I knew. I've been thinking that maybe the hunters got their hands on the pups, and in order to get them back, my brother tried to sacrifice your pack. Kill two birds with one stone. The hunters attack the pack and get what they want—to kill some wolf abominations—and in return Juneau gets the pups back?" He was only talking off the top of his head. "Another possibility is that he didn't know they had the pups, or he didn't really care, figuring he'd breed more. I don't even know if these are his children. They could be from any of my half brothers and sisters. I mean, as far as I know, my father sired at least two dozen children by almost as many women. He was like one of those ancient kings who surrounded himself with a harem and slept with a different woman every night." *The self-centered, useless pile of shit.* He kept that part to himself—after all, there were pups present.

"Do you think your brother is going to come looking for them?"

"I don't know what Juneau will do any longer. All of this has me confused and angry. He sent hunters here, people who would just as soon wipe him away as us."

"What if he didn't send them?" Denton asked. "What if they figured out that Juneau is a wolf, and they were following his people around to lead them to the packs?"

"That seems unlikely. Wolves would smell them too easily. We caught one and tracked them back to their camp, so other packs could as well. Juneau must have made a deal with the devil." How low could he sink? "I wish I had answers just as much as you do. But I don't."

Denton nodded. "The only thing that matters is that the pups are safe now."

One of them lifted his head and bared his teeth at Denton when he tried to stroke his head. Fredrik stopped walking, and Denton stared at the pup until he tilted his little head to the side. Then Denton lightly stroked both pups' heads.

"They need a lot of care," Fredrik said.

"I know," Denton said.

Fredrik shook his head. "It's more than that."

"How?" Christopher asked, clearly concerned.

"I'm trying to put my finger on it myself." He looked at the two of them. "Let's get back so I can think on it."

CHAPTER 4

THEY HURRIED back to the pack compound as quickly as they dared. Christopher was eventually able to take one of the pups from Fredrik. The pup whined for a minute, but he settled in Christopher's arms when he talked to him the same way Fredrik had.

By the time they arrived, everyone was starving, but food was waiting. Much to her chagrin, Catherine was taken directly to bed by Stan, and when she protested, Stan sent her a withering look the likes of which Christopher had never seen anyone, not even Mikael, give her. To his surprise, she backed down, and Stan led her away, carrying a plate of food. Christopher understood that feeling. His wolf needed to check Fredrik over. Christopher knew Fredrik was okay, but his wolf needed to know for himself.

Christopher was surprised at how hard it was to eat while holding a pup. He instantly gained a new respect for every single mother in the pack, including his own. He had never heard one of them complain. This was the hardest meal he'd ever eaten. The food on his plate ended up either down the front of him or in the pup's belly. Fredrik seemed to be having the same issue, but at least less food seemed to get knocked out of Fredrik's hand by the squirming, hungry pup.

"Now you know what I went through with each of you," his mother said with a completely unsympathetic grin. "How do you think I lost all my pregnancy weight? I didn't get to eat for three months."

"Mom," Christopher whined slightly.

She sat next to him. "Honey, that pup has been through a lot, and if he's willing to bond with you and try to trust you, that's a pretty amazing thing." She patted his shoulder. "And all I have to say is better you than me. I love my grandchildren, but I'm glad they all have mothers I can hand them to at the end of the day."

"Don't grump," Fredrik told him and then leaned closer.

Christopher forgot about his complaints when Fredrik got close, and he kissed his mate. That is, until the pup in his arms nipped at his jaw because he wasn't getting fed at that moment.

"Don't worry. After they eat, they'll tucker out, and we can put them to sleep."

"Famous last words," Christopher's mother muttered as she brought him more food. This time Christopher was able to eat more as the pup got full.

"What do you want to do with them?" Mikael asked from across the table. He was looking at Fredrik. "They're related to you, so I think it only fair that you act as their guardian."

Christopher hadn't thought of that, and he cringed. He wasn't sure how he felt about becoming an instant parent, or foster parent.

"We'll get them to bed and figure things out in the morning." Fredrik yawned, and the pup in his arms did the same. "I'd like it if they would shift. I'm not sure how old they are, but it would be good if they could talk."

Mikael looked at his mother, who shook her head. "They look to be about two, judging from their size. It can be hard to tell. If they haven't eaten regularly, they could be older. It depends how long they've been mistreated." She came over and gently cradled the pup out of Christopher's arms. "You are a sweet little one, aren't you?"

"Maybe, maybe not," Fredrik said, and everyone turned to him. He swallowed and looked sheepish. "We need to get these two someplace comfortable to sleep."

"They could join the other pups," Mikael suggested.

"I don't think so."

"What is it you aren't saying?" Christopher asked.

"Can we talk about it in the morning?" Fredrik asked.

Mikael agreed, and that put an end to the topic.

They finished eating, and both Christopher and Fredrik thanked his mother for the food and then walked back to the guest cabin, each with a pup in their arms. "Where are they going to sleep?"

"I thought I'd get a blanket and pillow and they could sleep on the floor near the bed. I think that's how they'll be happiest."

Christopher growled under his breath. His wolf wasn't happy at the moment. He wanted his mate alone and all to himself. "If you think so."

Fredrik set up a place for the pups, and they settled right together, curling up happily. They were warm and safe, and for now that seemed to be enough for them. Fredrik sat on the edge of the bed, watching them as they rolled around until they got comfortable and finally went to sleep.

"They're so cute," Christopher said.

"Yes, they are, but…."

"What did you mean earlier?" Christopher asked.

"They're related to me. They're likely my cousins." He sighed. "That means they have inside them what I have."

Christopher listened, definitely confused.

"There's this black place inside me. It's like I'm me most of the time, but there's also this darkness, like a hole that I can't see the bottom of. I've never liked it, so I keep that locked away. But sometimes, like when we were being shot at, it comes out. I heard Catherine's first cry and ignored it. I lay on the ground and didn't move."

"You were afraid," Christopher said. He certainly could understand that. "Who wouldn't be?"

Fredrik shook his head. "No, it was self-preservation. It was this part of me that welled up. I could feel it, saying I was more important and that if she died, she died. It was her fault for being careless."

"What?" Christopher's mouth flopped open.

"I can't explain it, but it kept me where I was until I heard her again."

"But you saved Catherine." He really didn't understand.

"I had to force those thoughts away, and then I could get up and get to Catherine. I was nearly too late. My battle with myself nearly cost her life. And...." Fredrik was clearly under stress, and Christopher sat next to him. "I don't know when it will come to the front. Like shooting their wounded leader, I never know. It's like there's this thing that lives inside, and I know what it is—it's that piece of my father that I can't seem to push out of my life. I inherited some of his blackness. We all did."

"Then why aren't you like the others?" Christopher asked.

"I'd like to think it's because I've fought against it for so long. My mother recognized it and told me I had to fight it with everything I had."

"We all have a bad side or selfish traits. No one is perfect."

"I know that. But this is different. I'm in control and I can fight it most of the time. But what if the pups are like my brothers? They never learned to control the darkness, so it took over. My father let it rule his life."

Christopher turned his gaze to the sleeping pups. "You said you fought it because of your mother. She treated you with love... right?"

"Yeah. She was the only one who did."

"Then maybe you need to teach them what your mother taught you. It could be that simple. If this darkness is inside you, then it's part of you. And now that you mention it, I can smell it. There's something pungent in your scent. It's just around the edges, and even to my wolf, it's barely there. I didn't know what it was."

Fredrik shrugged.

"That has to be it. Our scents are really complex. They're made up of everything in our lives. If you don't have enough food, then your scent changes because you're wasting away. If you're hurt or under stress, scared, happy, aroused—that's all reflected in our scent. So why wouldn't this be?"

"Okay. But what do we do?" Fredrik asked. "I'm not a parent. I don't know anything about raising pups."

Christopher pulled Fredrik into his arms and pressed him back on the bed. "I don't know. But we aren't going to find the answers tonight, and right now I need you more than I can say." He tugged at Fredrik's shirt, tossing it away once he got it off. "Maybe we should take a shower. I need the scent of that hunter off you. It's driving my wolf crazy." He took Fredrik by the hand, and they walked to the bathroom.

Fredrik started the shower as Christopher stripped, and then Fredrik did the same and followed Christopher under the water.

Christopher pushed Fredrik against the tile, licking, sucking, and nipping his way around his body so his wolf could be satisfied his mate was in one piece. The urge to claim Fredrik was great, his wolf pressing for him to take what was his. Christopher had to hold off. He stepped back. It was nearly physically painful to be away from Fredrik. Christopher washed himself quickly and started when Fredrik soaped his back.

"What did I do?" Fredrik asked.

"Nothing," Christopher said quickly. "It's hard for me to deny my wolf what he wants. You're his mate, and after being shot at and both of us being in danger, he's in an all-fired hurry to make you his."

"We can't. Not yet," Fredrik whispered.

"Why? We're the only mates either of us is going to get."

Fredrik stilled, his hands on Christopher's shoulders. "Because I can't saddle you forever with a mate who might have this blackness. I need to figure out what it is and what it truly means." Fredrik pressed against his back, and Christopher groaned softly, elongating the sound as Fredrik slid slick hands across his belly. "Let's not forget that my brother is still out there, and if he did send the hunters, then just because they failed doesn't mean that he's going to give up. You know it would be best for everyone in the pack if I took the pups and left."

"It wouldn't be best for me," Christopher countered, whirling around fast enough that he nearly lost his balance. "My mate, the only one I'll ever have, would be gone, and now that I've actually met you, I couldn't be happy with anyone else. Could you?" He had to stop his arms from crossing over his chest. Damn, he knew he was right, especially when Fredrik lowered his gaze. "I'll give you the time you need, but I'm not letting you go."

"Thank you," Fredrik said, putting his arms around Christopher's shoulders. "I've seen enough cruel and mean things to last the rest of my life. I won't be the source of them for anyone." He shivered even though the water was hot. "I couldn't bear it if anything happened to this pack because of me."

Christopher closed his eyes and held Fredrik tighter. "You aren't responsible for Juneau's actions. You did what you had to in order to escape and stop him from hurting someone close to everyone in this pack. We are more than capable of standing up to whomever we have to. Now, let's finish this shower so we can go to bed."

"The pups are out there," Fredrik murmured.

"Okay," Christopher whispered and turned off the water. "Put your hands on the wall."

"Huh?"

"Put your hands on the wall," Christopher repeated, and when Fredrik complied, he parted his legs. Fuck, Fredrik looked beautiful like that, standing still, waiting for him. "That's it." Christopher pressed to him, cock sliding along Fredrik's cheeks, sending quivers of delight that electrified him.

"Chris…." Fredrik moaned, and Christopher pressed closer, wrapping his arms around him and slipping his hands over Fredrik's chest, tweaking his nipples, sliding them lower over Fredrik's belly. Christopher ran his fingers through his soft nest of curls before circling them around his cock, earning a growl that filled the small space. "No teasing."

"I'd never tease you. My mate deserves so much better than that." Christopher tempted fate and sucked on Fredrik's shoulder, raising a few marks. He stayed away from his neck to avoid further temptation and had to stop altogether as his canines lengthened and his vision shifted to black and white. His cock ached, and Christopher had to stop his wolf from plunging in to take his mate right now. Fredrik deserved more. He calmed his wolf by saying it would happen soon enough, but his beast was impatient.

"I want you now!" Fredrik whimpered, grinding back against him.

"You're going to bring out the animal in me."

"If I wanted a kitten, I'd have found a house cat. I want your wolf. He's part of what I love about you." He shivered. "God," he whined loudly, voice going high when Christopher gripped his cock hard.

Christopher bent his knees, sliding down his mate's back, nipping gently until he reached his ass. Then he spread his cheeks and dove in. He didn't have lube, so he figured he'd do this the old-fashioned way, the wolf way. He licked, sucked, and probed, the taste of his mate strong and rich, with a hint of soap.

Fredrik rested his head on the tile, mewling softly. "I don't want to yell, but I'm so damn close."

Christopher stood, spit to wet his cock, and slid close, pressing into his mate's viselike heat. It took all he had not to come. He was instantly on the edge, his wolf so keyed up that if he gave away control for a second, there would be no stopping. "Feels so good," he breathed.

"Yeah." Fredrik gripped him tightly, sending zings of pleasure flying all through him.

"Keep that up and it's going to be over."

Fredrik's legs shook. "I'm not going to last anyway. You have me too keyed up, and my wolf wants your wolf to fuck me like there's no tomorrow."

Christopher surged forward, sandwiching Fredrik between him and the tile. That was all he needed to hear. His wolf took over, and Christopher pounded into Fredrik, holding on to just enough control to keep from claiming him with a bite. If he did that, they'd mate permanently, and dammit, he did not want that without Fredrik's permission. That was all that held him back.

They were trying not to be too loud, but they were failing. Not that this was going to last long. He felt like a teenager, and his climax barreled through him way too soon.

Fredrik tensed around him, groaning loudly. As soon as he felt Fredrik start to come, Christopher followed right behind, holding the wall to keep himself upright while he held on to what little control he had left.

Neither of them moved until Fredrik began sliding down the tile. Christopher groaned when they separated and then grabbed Fredrik, holding him upright as they caught their breath. Then, once he could think, he turned on the water and moved them under, letting it sluice over them to send their sweat down the drain.

"You know I'm going to smell like you inside and out."

"That's the whole idea."

"So maybe next time, you should smell like me."

Christopher figured Fredrik was testing the waters, and he stiffened. He'd never considered turning the tables. The guys he'd been with had always been happy to bottom, and he was more than thrilled to top. "If you like." He wasn't sure how comfortable he was with it, but this was his mate and he wasn't going to deny him anything.

"We'll see." Fredrik plunged his head under the water, rinsing out his hair. "I don't want you to be uncomfortable, and the idea clearly makes you that."

"Hey. I know you'll make it good."

Fredrik nestled to him. "I've had the best teacher."

For a split second, jealousy spiked, and then, *duh*, Christopher realized Fredrik was talking about him. He grinned and turned off the water, still holding Fredrik while they dripped dry. Finally, when he could bear to let go, Christopher pushed the curtain aside and got the towels. They dried themselves and got out of the shower.

He was clean and satiated for the moment. His mate wore his marks, and he was fine. Christopher's wolf was delighted. That happiness lasted until he opened the door and stepped out. The pillow the pups had been sleeping on was torn, with stuffing scattered everywhere. "What happened?" He sniffed and let his nose lead him to the chair in the corner.

"We must have scared them," Fredrik said. "I need to learn to be quieter."

"Don't you dare," he said as gently as he could. Christopher loved that Fredrik was loud and willing to tell him what he liked. There was nothing sexier or more passionate, in his opinion, than a vocal lover, and thinking of the sounds Fredrik made was almost enough to get him going again. Except this was not the time to think about things like that. Not with two small pups cowering in the corner under a chair. He needed to get his mind off his dick and onto what was truly important.

"It's all right," Fredrik cooed and got down on the floor. "No one was being hurt. I'm sorry we were making noise." He gently pulled first one and then the second pup out, cradling them to his bare skin. "You have nothing to be afraid of here." He lifted his gaze. "They're shivering, and their little hearts are racing like mad."

Christopher lifted one of the pups and gently stroked his fluffball coat. "Is it possible that they heard a lot of yelling and screaming? Maybe even rough sex where someone got hurt?"

"Anything is possible in my family," Fredrik said in a soft tone, keeping the anger out of it. He climbed into bed, still cradling the pup to him.

"They can't sleep with us," Christopher said, without heat. He didn't want to add to their stress, but he wasn't sharing a bed with his mate and two pups. "Put him here with me," he said, unable to fight the look in Fredrik's eyes. "The two of them will curl together, and then you can clean up the mess and they'll go back to sleep in their mini pup pile. Tomorrow we'll see if we can coax them into their human forms. They're going to have to get used to it."

Fredrik gaped at him. "These little ones have been traumatized to the point that some noise from the bathroom scared them. They were in a cage for who knows how long and treated as dogs. They may think they're dogs, and it's going to take time for them to come around."

Christopher sat on the edge of the bed, putting the pups together. "They may not have a lot of time. They could be staying as pups because their human side was traumatized. If that's the case, then if they don't shift back, they may lose that part of themselves. You and I don't think that way, but if their wolf is that strong because their human side doesn't want to come out…." He didn't want to finish the sentence.

"They'll lead a half life."

"Yeah. But I think it's too soon to draw any conclusions." He stood and then leaned over the bed to kiss Fredrik gently. "I'm going to clean up the mess, and then we'll go to bed. For one night, they can sleep where they're happy. But tomorrow we are definitely going to get with Mikael. His alphaness may be able to help them."

Christopher got a broom from the kitchen, along with a trash bag, and scooped the stuffing into the bag. He'd see if anyone could use the material before throwing it away. He put everything away when he was done, and by the time he returned, Fredrik had curled under the covers with the pups pressed to his chest, all three of them asleep. The pups had their heads tucked under their paws, and they looked so sweet. Christopher turned out the lights and got into bed, finding what little room there was left. The pups were definitely bed pigs, especially as soon as they found out what Christopher wanted. Then they spread out, backs pressed to Fredrik, legs toward him, and applied a good dose of nails whenever he got too close.

It was well into the night before one of the pups rolled over and pressed to him. Within minutes he was asleep.

CHRISTOPHER YAWNED for the millionth time since getting up. He'd had eight cups of coffee—he *was* counting—and all he did was pee and still yawn. His mother had to have substituted decaffeinated coffee. He should be wired, even with his wolf metabolism. Still, he wanted to help work on the cabin that he'd been told would be his. So he slogged through and pushed his fatigue aside.

Fredrik stayed with the pups and helped when he could. Mostly he got things with the two little balls of fur following after him like he'd disappear forever if they let him out of their sight. "Do you need more coffee?" Fredrik asked as he wiped his brow.

"No, I'm okay." They had finished the last of the walls and were putting on the roof slats so they could shingle and then start work on the interior. It was all hands on deck at this point.

"What will you do for furniture when the cabin is done? You can't have much," Fredrik inquired.

"I'll make it," Jerry said. "I did a lot of the furniture in the main house and other cabins. Well, I design it, and a lot of the men and I work to make it. Stan is really great with his hands, and so are some of the younger boys. It's fun for all of us." Jerry attached the board, and Fredrik handed up the next one.

"Can we help?" Alexi asked, his brother standing next to him. Both were eagerly staring up at the roof.

"Yes. You can gather up all the little pieces of wood and put them in a pile right here," Mikael said. "We can burn some of them and others we can reuse."

"Okay," they answered and got to work. Their mother, Anna, joined them, as did some of the other women, and progress picked up quickly.

It felt good to be working, and after a while, the sun grew higher in the sky. Living in an area where it could snow any month of the year, it always felt amazing when the sun shone.

Christopher peeled off his shirt and went back to work. The last of the stringer boards was in place, and with the roof covered, they began shingling. "Why don't we use regular asphalt shingles?" Christopher asked.

Mikael looked up from where he was sealing between some of the logs. "They're expensive and they never break down. If we used them, we'd be up to our ears in garbage. So we used cedar shakes and replace them when needed. It's better for our environment."

Christopher nodded and gave his brother a quick salute. Then Jerry called him over and demonstrated exactly how the shingles had to be attached. It was a process of overlapping each shingle so it covered the gap of the one under it.

"Stan is an expert at splitting each one off the logs we gathered," Jerry said, pointing to where he was working. "He's the possible bottleneck. We can set them faster than he can split them. So that's why he started a while ago."

"You have this down to a science."

"This is the third cabin we've built. The pack keeps growing, so we build, but not too big, and we spread them out enough so there is privacy but close enough for shared shelter, especially in the winter."

Christopher got to work, and after an hour of driving nails, his arms ached like they never had before. The hammer got heavier by the second, but he and Jerry continued working.

"Take a break," Jerry said after a while, and Christopher was grateful.

He climbed down and sat on the ground. Fredrik sat next to him, covered in sawdust and dirt. He handed him some water, and the pups climbed onto Fredrik's lap, curling together. "Have they stood still at all?"

"No. They race around my legs and tussle with each other, but they never get far away from me."

"They're bonding with you," Catherine explained as she joined them. "They've decided they're safe with you, and they've imprinted on your scent."

"I know I've been caring for them, but…."

Catherine put her hand on Fredrik's shoulder, and Christopher wanted to bat it away. He growled regardless, and Catherine growled right back, and then she ignored him and turned to Fredrik. "I'm wondering if they're orphans. You told Mikael they were relatives, and the black eyes are unusual. Are you aware of any of your relatives dying?"

"It happened all the time. One cousin kills another in order to rise in the pack. Challenges are to the death. Why?"

"Because in essence they've adopted you. They wouldn't do that this quickly if their mother was still alive. They're lone wolves and they know it, so they've latched tightly onto you."

"So they think I'm their parent?" Fredrik said.

"Yes."

"What do I do?"

"You need to decide if you want to be a parent. If not, then you'll need to distance yourself from them in order to allow them to imprint on someone else." Catherine gently stroked the pup's head that rested on his right knee.

"We don't even know their names."

"I told him we need to try to get them to shift," Christopher said, and he was grateful when Catherine agreed.

"Talk them through it. I have a feeling if you get one to shift, the other will follow."

Fredrik lifted one pup into his arms, meeting his eyes. It was so cute. The pup kept batting at Fredrik's ears. "Stop that," he said gently. "I need you to shift for me. You need to think about being a child again. I'm here, and so is Christopher. No one is going to hurt you. Can you do that for me?"

The pup blinked at him and then swiped a paw over his chin. Christopher tried with the other pup but got the same response. They squirmed to get down and ran around, batting at each other for a while before curling up once again in Fredrik's lap.

Christopher had to go back to work, so he stood and felt Fredrik's gaze on his back as he walked away and climbed the ladder. He turned and shared a look with Fredrik and wondered at how quickly his life could change. He'd found his mate, and now there was the complexity of two pups that had to be thought about as well.

Christopher forced his mind back onto his work in order to push away the weight of responsibility that seemed to be falling around him.

"You need to keep your mind on your work," Jerry chided as Christopher nearly pounded his hand along with the nail. That was the third time in twenty minutes. "Whatever you're chewing on can wait until you're not on a roof. Falling off will hurt even a shifter." Jerry smiled, and Christopher went back to work, keeping his hands and his mind where they belonged.

As the day drew to a close, they all worked faster. The roof was nearly shingled, and that meant just a few more tasks and the house would be tight against the elements. Then he understood the work would shift to outfitting and finishing.

"Good job today," Mikael said as they gathered their tools for the night. Jerry had just pounded the last nail home, securing the last shingle.

Christopher felt as though he'd sweated out five pounds by the time he climbed off the roof and got back on the ground. "Where are the pups?" he asked Fredrik, who turned to the side. Denton lay on the ground, with both pups jumping and playing around him.

"He's going to see if he can get them to shift. First he says he needs to get their trust."

"I think he just wanted pups to play with," Mikael said from behind them, with Stephan following him.

"Are things good?" Fredrik asked, glancing at Stephan and then back at Mikael.

"I think that's up to you," Mikael said, staring at him.

It took a second for Christopher to realize that Mikael meant him. He was waiting, and Christopher had to give him an answer. It would have been so easy to say Stephan couldn't stay. He had eyes for Fredrik; there was little doubt about that. Just the way he was looking at him now got Christopher's blood boiling, and he wanted to step sideways to block Stephan's view.

"Let's walk a minute," Mikael said. He tilted his head to the side and then led them away from the others toward the woods.

"Why me? You make the decisions for the pack," Christopher said.

"I do?" Mikael turned around. "I lead the pack so that each member can be happy and make the best use of their talents. I didn't decide where to build the cabin we're building for you—Jerry did. All I did was approve it."

"And that makes you responsible for the decision."

"That's what a leader does. And that's why I couldn't make you the leader of the pack that needed one. You aren't ready for that. The pack would suffer because you'd feel you needed to do everything yourself in order for it to be right. And you can't do that. You also have to make tough decisions, like the one I'm giving you right now. Yes, I know."

"Do you think he's a threat?"

"To the pack? No. I could be wrong, because no one is ever right all the time, but I'm convinced he wants to join our pack and that he'll be a productive member. I don't sense any duplicity in him. I think he was able to fool Fredrik's brother into thinking he was loyal to him, and then as soon as he was away, he decided to make a break for it. I can't blame him. Can you?"

Christopher shook his head. "This is home and it's a good one."

"Yes, it is," Mikael agreed. "What do you want to do?"

Christopher knew this was a test of sorts, and he didn't want to fail. "Then he should stay. We haven't turned away people we could help before. Why should we start now? But if he comes for my mate, he and I are going to have a problem."

Mikael turned, and Christopher followed his gaze and saw Stephan staring off toward the pack house. Christopher followed his gaze. "I think he's found someone he finds much more interesting anyway."

"Kaiawa?"

"Could be. Don't know if anything will come of it, but there's interest there. Maybe it's more and maybe it's not." Mikael patted him on the shoulder.

"You knew that before you asked me, didn't you?" Christopher asked.

Mikael smiled. "And you made a good decision before you knew. That's what counts. Follow what's in your heart. That's what I did, and let me tell you, Denton made me work hard for what I wanted. But I always knew."

Christopher turned to where Fredrik was now playing with the pups. That weight returned, and now he knew its name. *Responsibility.* Something he hadn't taken into account when he'd asked Mikael to make him a pack leader. Now he felt it, especially looking at those pups. Catherine had said they were already imprinting on Fredrik, and those pups needed family, the same as everyone else. Fredrik was as close to family as they had, and Christopher wasn't going to ask him to give them up. "I owe you such a huge apology," Christopher said without looking away.

"What for?"

"Being completely clueless," Christopher answered without taking his gaze off his mate.

Fredrik rolled back, the pups jumping on his chest, bounding around him, yips and barks of happiness floating over to him.

"Go on and join them," Mikael said. "But I need everyone to stay close to the compound, and I'll need you to help patrol the borders tomorrow. Karl is out right now, and Kaiawa will be going out later. I have a bad feeling," Mikael added in a voice just loud enough for Christopher's wolf hearing to pick up.

"How do you know?"

"I just do," Mikael added and then walked away.

Christopher watched Mikael go, his shoulders a little slumped, like he wasn't walking quite as tall as he usually did. Denton approached him. Christopher wasn't sure if they said anything to each other, but Mikael seemed taller and less worried after just a few seconds. They continued on, and Christopher went back and joined Fredrik and the pups, feeling more and more like he belonged here all the time.

THE HEAT of the day didn't dissipate, and as dusk fell, a breeze blew up, adding humidity and discomfort to the air. Maybe Mikael had been right. Clouds had been forming for a while, and they blotted out the sun before its time. "We need to get everything inside," Christopher told Fredrik as the first gusts of wind blew through the compound, sending some of the lighter chairs tumbling. "Take the pups in, and I'll help out here. Keep them calm."

"Should we go to the pack house?"

"That's up to you. Whatever you think is going to make them feel best." He stroked both pups, who whined at Fredrik's feet. "It's going to be okay. Stay with Fredrik, and he'll make sure you're both safe." Another gust of wind, stronger than before, swirled menacingly around them.

"Everyone, put things away," Catherine told her children. "We may not have much time before this hits."

"I'll be in as soon as I can," Christopher told Fredrik.

"Have you seen Kaiawa?" Stephan asked, almost skidding to a stop near them.

"I think he was out checking the pack borders. Go on up to the pack house and ask Alpha Mikael. He'll know."

Stephan nodded and took off at a run while Christopher got busy with the others, battening down anything that was loose. Once he was done, he hurried over to the cabin under construction. It was the most vulnerable building at this point, but the windows were in and so was the door. Whether that would give it the strength to survive a storm, only time would tell.

Christopher walked the outside of the building. He picked up a few stray boards and other things that might blow around, and put them inside. Once he was done, he hurried back toward the pack house, meeting Jerry as he did. "I put things away around the new cabin."

"I was just going over to check." They walked together to the main house and climbed the steps to the deck. "What the hell is that?" Jerry asked, pointing toward the horizon and down across the valley below.

"Looks like clouds touching the ground."

"But it's inside the valley, and they're black."

"You've got really good eyes." Now that Jerry mentioned it, he could see whatever had dipped toward the ground was getting blacker and more ominous by the second.

The door slid open and closed behind them. "Are you watching that?" Mikael asked.

"Yeah," Christopher said and let Jerry explain what they'd seen. "Do you know what it means?"

Mikael shook his head. "But it isn't good. Let's get everyone inside now. I have a feeling this storm is going to get very nasty." Hearing fear in Mikael's voice was something very unusual.

Christopher sprang into action. He hurried down the steps and helped the pack get the last of the outdoor things inside and locked away. Most headed to the pack house, but Christopher went to the guest cabin, where Fredrik and the pups were. He pulled open the door as a gust of wind blew inside, acting like it was alive and looking for something. He slammed the door closed, and the wind continued for a second before dying away.

Fredrik came out of the bedroom, wide-eyed and shaking. "This isn't just a storm."

"Then what is it?"

"My brother," Fredrik said.

"I don't understand." He hurried to Fredrik and took him in his arms. "What's going on?"

"The darkness I told you about isn't just made up of black emotions like anger. It allows us, or some of us, to harness the darker forces of nature."

"Are you saying your brother made this storm?" Christopher asked.

"No. He isn't that powerful. My father might have been at one time, but Juneau isn't. But he could use a storm and make it worse or direct its wrath toward a specific point."

"Like at us?"

"Exactly. This storm was already powerful enough because of the heat and humidity, but if he adds his own power to it, all that intensity will be centered here."

"How?"

"I don't know. I was always afraid to use that power. My mother said it was bad, and that if I did, I'd turn out to be like my father. Since I didn't want that to happen, I never tried."

"What do we do?"

Fredrik shrugged. "I have no idea other than to hunker down and try to weather it out."

The pups whined, and Fredrik let go and returned to the bedroom. Christopher followed, and they each held one as the windows rattled with the first pelting of rain.

It got worse by the second. The windows showed only sheets of water running outside them, and they rattled from the force of the unrelenting wind, which only seemed to grow. The pups knew things were getting bad, and the one in Christopher's arms tried to burrow beneath his shirt. He was nervous as well and sat next to Fredrik.

"This can't last very long. Not something this intense." He shared a look with Fredrik and continued to try to comfort the pups as the storm grew worse.

"She needs my help," Fredrik said all of a sudden and placed the second pup into Christopher's arms.

"What? Who needs your help?" Christopher set both pups on the bed and jumped to try to stop Fredrik as he hurried toward the door.

"I don't know who she is, but she says she needs my help. That I'm the only one." Fredrik seemed confused, and Christopher wondered if the storm was getting to him and if he should try to keep him close in hope of calming him.

"What voice?" Christopher was completely confused as to what Fredrik was talking about, but he was nearly frantic and energy rolled off him.

"Please stay here with them." Fredrik indicated the pups. "I have to try to help her save all of us." He was jittery, and he seemed to be listening for something.

"Who is she?" Christopher asked.

"I don't know." He hurried toward the front of the cabin. "But she keeps telling me that she needs my help to save all of us."

Fredrik was going out in the storm, and that wasn't a good idea. The wind was so fierce that he could be blown over or injured by flying debris.

"But I don't hear anything." This was way beyond strange.

"I know. Apparently I'm the only one who hears her, and I hope I'm not completely crazy to be listening to this voice that seems to be in my head." He paused. "Okay, I know there isn't much time." His eyes were a little vacant, and Christopher knew Fredrik wasn't speaking to him. "I don't know what's going to happen." Fredrik pulled open the front door and stepped out. He was immediately drenched even before he could yank the door closed.

Christopher stared at the door, wondering what the hell had just happened and if he would ever see his mate again.

CHAPTER 5

THE WIND danced around in a frenzy; rain pummeled the earth as though it were filled with anger and needed to release it on everything it touched. Hate, pain, and rage filled the air around him, spreading in every direction, black as the night and unpredictable as a stampede.

"I'm here." He had to be completely crazy to be outside in this weather. The rain hurt where it hit his skin, but he did his best to ignore it.

The worst of the storm is coming—a vortex that will take everything the pack has. There are limits to what I can do. But you have the power.

"How?"

Push the twister north and then back around in a circle. It will fall in on itself.

"How do I do that?" He had never used that power inside him. He was afraid to now.

The power you have isn't good or bad. It just is. The intention with which you use it is what matters. You must concentrate and push the entire storm away. Feel its core of power and push against it.

"I can't do that." Fredrik was soaked to the bone and shivering in wet clothes that clung to him in places while whipping behind him where they were loose.

Yes, you can.

"Who are you?" Fredrik asked.

You know who I am. You've already felt me. At the cave. There isn't much time. You must try to save my children.

Fredrik let go of the part of himself he'd always kept locked away and hadn't dared release. As soon as he did, he felt the storm and the power locked inside it. The core was just to the west and coming closer by the second. Fredrik did what she told him, pressing against it, but the storm was too powerful. Fredrik concentrated harder, pushing once again, this time with more force.

The power within the storm pushed back. He could feel his brother wrapped up in it. Fredrik pressed harder, letting everything he'd kept bottled up free, picturing Juneau, throwing him away. He kept up, feeling movement where before there had been none.

The storm moved faster now, going north, away from them. The rain still fell in sheets, but the wind slackened. The power within the storm remained the same, however. It didn't waver. Somehow, deep down inside, Fredrik knew he had to break the source of that power. He pushed once again, adding momentum to move the storm back onto itself.

It wasn't enough, and he was tiring. There had to be more he could do. He couldn't keep this up for much longer. He continued pushing, this time sending the storm back the way it had come, toward his brother. Something snapped, like a twig stepped on in the woods. The dark, foreign power inside the storm disappeared and the winds subsided. The rain settled down to a normal pace, falling lightly around him.

Fredrik fell to his knees and then collapsed on the soaked ground. He heard footsteps splash toward him, but he was too tired to get up.

"Sweetheart," Christopher said, trying to get him up on his feet. Fredrik's legs wouldn't hold his weight, no matter what he did. Christopher lifted him into his arms, and Fredrik held him around the neck and was soon inside, the wind and rain instantly quieting as the door closed.

"Where are the pups?"

"On the bed." Christopher took him through to the bathroom and pulled off his clothes. He was nearly as wet as Fredrik, and they ended up both stripped to the skin, with Christopher touching and checking over every inch of him. Then Christopher got some clothes, swaddled Fredrik in a pair of sweatpants and a T-shirt, and led him to the bed.

The pups curled around him as soon as he lay down, both of them getting as close as they could. "Were you afraid?" he asked the pups softly. "I'm okay. Just really tired," he added to reassure them.

Christopher stroked his forehead. "What happened out there and who was this voice you said you heard?"

"I'm not sick or crazy. I heard this voice when I first got here and then again in the cave. She made fun of Alpha Mikael, saying that he was long-winded."

"Oh my...," Christopher muttered.

"She told me there was only so much she could do, and that I needed to use what I'd always kept bottled up to help her children."

"It was the Mother," Christopher whispered. "Mom said that she had spoken to Mikael before, but I'm not aware of her speaking directly to others."

Fredrik breathed deeply; what little energy he had left was fading quickly. "She told me what to do, and I did what she said. But I need to sleep."

"I'll get you some food." Christopher hurried away as Fredrik closed his eyes.

He was asleep instantly, and when Christopher woke him, he ate the eggs and toast that he'd brought before going right back to sleep.

FREDRIK HAD no idea how long he was out. The windows were dark and he was alone in the bed when he woke. He still felt weak but had to get out of the bed. He used the bathroom and then padded into the other room, where he found Christopher and the pups playing on the floor.

"I tried getting them to shift again, but they weren't interested," Christopher said.

"They're having way too much fun as pups. There's days of play and sleep. They have sharp teeth they can use to fend off anyone who might hurt them…."

"You think they might have been abused or something?"

"It's possible," Fredrik said, sitting on the sofa and letting the pups settle on his lap. "We'll have to get Mikael to help us. I think he's the only one they might respond to." They whined, and he chuckled. "They already have us wrapped around their paws, so they have no real imperative to change at the moment."

"Do you need something to eat?"

"Yeah. I'm starved," Fredrik said. "A steak or something like that would be great." He had a craving for red meat. His energy levels still seemed very low, and food, followed by more sleep, was definitely in order. "What time is it?"

"Almost eleven."

Fredrik settled back on the sofa, content. "Is it still raining?"

"No. The storm blew itself out pretty soon after you went to bed, and now it's clear with a ceiling of stars."

The sear of beef reached his ears and nose. Fredrik salivated, and the pups perked up their heads.

"This is for Fredrik. I made you dinner a while ago."

Fredrik motioned Christopher to come over. "Do we have some more beef?"

"Yeah."

"If you want some, boys, you need to shift so we can make sure you're old enough. Only big boys get to eat steak like that." He winked at Christopher.

Both pups growled low in their throats. It still came out pup-sounding, but it was much more menacing than before.

"You need to picture yourself as a boy and shift back." He kept his voice firm and waited. "Get two blankets."

Christopher hurried away.

"I mean it. You can have some steak if you shift." He wasn't above bribery.

The pup to his right crawled off his lap and slowly began to shift. Even though he was small, it took longer for him to shift because of his age. Shifting speed often depended more on strength and experience than size. But when he did, a naked boy—Fredrik guessed he was between three and four—lay on the sofa. "That's good."

Christopher returned and wrapped the boy in a light blanket. The other pup, after seeing his brother, must have decided he was hungry, because he shifted as well. Christopher handed Fredrik a blanket, and Fredrik wrapped the second—twin—brother. "You hold them. I'm going to make sure the food doesn't burn and call Catherine and my mother to get them some clothes."

"Do you have names?" Fredrik asked.

"He Pietro."

"He Nate," the other one answered.

Fredrik thought it cute that they answered for each other. Fredrik cuddled both of them and couldn't wipe the smile off his face. "How old are you?"

"Free," Nate answered.

"Three and a half," Pietro clarified.

He wasn't sure if he should ask about their mother, but he decided against it for now.

"My mother is on her way over," Christopher said as he came back into the room. "She said she has some clothes."

"Did you hear that? Grandma is on her way," Fredrik said with excitement, and both boys stared at him as if he were from outer space. "Once you get dressed, the food will be ready."

The door opened and Christopher's mother rushed in, all smiles. She lifted Pietro and cooed over him like he was the center of the world. Nate whined, and she set Pietro down and crooned the same way over him. "Now let's get you boys dressed," she gushed and stepped back.

The boys let the blankets fall away, and they each took one of her hands.

Fredrik covered his mouth as he watched Christopher's mother leading two naked little boys toward the bedroom. He realized she'd left the bag with the boys' clothes, so he brought it to her and helped her dress the two pups, who acted like they would much rather be naked. By the way the boys squirmed and fought them, Fredrik thought they might be better off letting them run around in nothing.

"They have to learn," Christopher's mother told him. "The sooner they do, the easier it will be on them and everyone." She lifted a dressed Pietro. "Come on, young man, let's get you in the kitchen for something to eat." That ended the fighting.

Christopher had the food ready, the boys' beef cut into small pieces. Christopher took Nate, and his mother helped Pietro. Both boys ate like they hadn't had dinner just a few hours before.

"What happened to these babies?" she asked as Pietro nearly took her fingers in his haste to take a bite.

"I don't know, and I'm not sure we'll ever find out," Fredrik said. "I don't intend to try to speak to my brother, but maybe Stephan would know." He made a note to talk to him in the morning.

Finally both boys seemed full, and they yawned. "I'll take these two and put them to bed in the other bedroom," Christopher's mother said. "They'll probably sleep through the night now." She was grinning from ear to ear, and the boys went with her readily when she herded them toward the second bedroom. "I brought you pajamas to wear to bed, but you have to stay in human form. Can you do that for me?"

"Always?" Pietro looked down. "I wanna be a wolfie too."

"You can. Tomorrow afternoon with the other kids, you can both be wolfies, and we can see if your cousins will teach you to play pounce." She laughed. "And maybe we can get Christopher to be the antelope." She chuckled, and then the door closed, cutting off the remainder of her conversation.

Fredrik sighed. The boys would be okay, eventually, but he knew there would be other hurdles. At that moment, when he was filled with doubt and feeling overwhelmed, Christopher took his hand.

"I don't know what's going to happen next," Christopher said. "The last few days have had more ups and downs than the mountains that surround us. But we'll figure it out together."

Fredrik closed his eyes and tried to slow the swirling inside his head. It had started during the storm and continued no matter what he did. "I'll try. But something is different. It's like something has changed inside me. When I fought the storm, I set something loose that I can't put back in its box."

"I don't understand," Christopher said.

"I know. No one can. It's inside. I feel this power that wasn't there before." He crackled as it swirled around inside him, becoming stronger and stronger with each revolution. "I think I understand what was inside my father and my brother." The energy swirls were visible behind his eyes. "I want it to stop. It needs to."

"You let it out during the storm, so try to put it back where it was." Christopher stroked his arm and then enfolded him in a deep hug.

"Why aren't you afraid of me? Because you should be. What if I can't control this and it comes out of me or drives me crazy?" That could have been what happened to his father. Fredrik's mother had always said the Anton she first met was not the same person he became later in life. She said he changed, and maybe this was the source of that change. Maybe his father had used the power inside and found he couldn't put it back, and afterward it ate at him. He didn't know, but he could imagine that happening.

"You'd never hurt me," Christopher said just above a whisper, then kissed him, sliding his tongue between his lips and pressing him back onto the sofa. "Stop thinking about what happened and what you can do."

"How?"

"Just think about me." Christopher stroked his chest and belly. "Think about how I make you feel and channel your energy into that. Let go of the swirls and this whole thing that I can't understand. Because it doesn't matter. Not to me. All that does is you. I knew that the first time I saw you."

"How can you know that? Or that I can control this… thing?" Fredrik wanted to run and never look back. He had brought pain and suffering to Christopher and his pack. He was sure his brother was behind the storm and its behavior.

"Because you're my mate. The only one I am ever going to have, and as my mate, you're my other half. If you have this power, then I'm supposed to help you learn to control it, or counterbalance it somehow. That's how things work."

"Who told you that?"

I did.

Fredrik sat up. That voice was back. He listened but heard no more.

The bedroom door opened, and Christopher's mother came out, smiling shyly at them as she walked to the door. "I think the two of you should probably take whatever it is you're doing to your bedroom. You'll be more comfortable."

"Mom," Christopher whined.

"Please. Like I don't know what you two were doing, or getting ready to do. I did have four children, after all. I know what sex is and how to do it howlingly well. If I do say so myself." She chuckled, and Fredrik had to join her when Christopher blushed beet red. "You think you invented sex." She rolled her eyes and shook her head. "I miss your father every single day, but there are times I wish a man would come along and sweep me off my paws."

"Good God, Mom. I think you just killed the mood forever."

"Piffle," she said. "Don't be a prude. It isn't attractive." With that, she pulled open the door and left the cabin.

Christopher sighed when she closed the door. "I'm sorry."

"Why? I think she and my mother would have been best friends. If my mother were still alive, she would have done her best to embarrass me as well." He felt lighter now that his mind and focus weren't on what was going on inside his own head. "Your mother is a wise woman, and I think that you and I should follow her advice."

"As long as you can keep it down so we don't scare the pups again."

"Me? That was all your fault."

Christopher moved closer, and instantly heat rose in Fredrik. Damn, all he needed to do was stand near Christopher and his mind went blank. Fredrik forgot about storms and swirls of energy. All he could think about was Christopher and how his hands would feel as soon as they touched him. He swallowed hard and waited while Christopher turned out the lights, then followed him into the bedroom.

He had no choice. Christopher called to him. Once the door closed, Christopher pressed Fredrik against it and lifted his arms over his head, then kissed him hard enough to buckle his knees. He would have ended up on the floor if Christopher hadn't stopped him from falling and then lifted him off his feet and carried him to the bed.

"In case you have any doubt, I want you. No one else. You are mine and I'm yours. Things will change around us, and it seems you have two pups who have attached themselves to you."

"That's a lot for anyone—"

"It doesn't matter. Things will change. But you and I, my mate? You and I are forever. That's all that counts. I will care for and love those pups because they are part of your family and thus your life. Do you understand?"

"Yeah, I think I do."

"My mom nearly died when my father went. Only her considerable strength kept her from giving up. They were mates and one of the best pairs I ever saw. I was lucky to have had them as parents. And that's what I want."

"What about your place in the pack?"

"I realize now that it will come. I didn't think I fit in anywhere, but I fit with you, and everything else doesn't seem to matter as much. So as soon as the other cabin is done, you and I will move in there, and we'll bring the pups and anyone else you want along with us, as long as I get to do this each and every night." Christopher quickly and thoroughly divested them of their clothes, his eyes wide and carnal as he moved.

Fredrik chuckled when his shirt ended up on the bedside lamp, but Christopher kissed him, and Fredrik forgot about everything else. Christopher's solid weight on top of him and the earthy taste of his mate as he plundered his lips pretty much shut down Fredrik's ability to think about anything else.

Maybe Christopher was right and they were mates because they were what the other needed. His mind had quickly settled, and the swirls of energy and his worry about containing it were gone, forgotten in the haze of Christopher's caresses, which seemed to reach deep down into him. Sex had been fun the few times he'd had it before meeting Christopher, but it had also been a source of worry. With Christopher, it was different. Everything seemed right, exactly as it should be.

"Chris…," Fredrik cried and put a hand over his mouth, biting the pad slightly when Christopher sucked him deep.

"No talking," Christopher said. "You have to be quiet. So as long as you are, I'll keep going. But as soon as you make a sound, I stop." He smiled. "Can you do that?"

Fredrik opened his mouth and then snapped it shut. He nodded, and Christopher sucked him once again. Since he hadn't said anything about moving, Fredrik thrust upward, and Christopher took it. Within seconds, Fredrik was out of his mind, thrusting and fucking Christopher's mouth. The intense heat and pressure were lovely and made his head swim. All his attention and focus centered on where Christopher touched him. He swore if the cabin walls fell around them, he'd hardly notice. This was all that mattered—being with Christopher at this very moment. He wanted to tell him to suck him and let loose a steady stream of moans and groans, but he held it in and went with the tingling feeling that crawled up and down his back. God, this was damn near torture, and he loved every second of it.

His eyes watered and he stiffened as the pressure built. He wanted to warn Christopher, but he didn't want him to stop either. Fredrik ended up fisting the sheets, clamping his eyes closed and trying to control his own body. It was a totally lost cause as he tumbled into his release, mouth dropping open in a silent cry of ecstatic wonder.

Christopher let him slip from between his lips and kissed him. Fredrik tasted his own flavor in Christopher's mouth and on his talented tongue. "I want you so bad," Christopher whispered.

"You have me," Fredrik said. There was no place in the world that he'd rather be. So when Christopher reached for the lube, prepared him, and then slowly, teasingly, slid into him, he gasped and tried with all his might to be as quiet as possible. The stretch, the way he was filled, just being with his mate, nearly overwhelmed him. Fredrik had never had the urge to bite anyone, even as a pup, but Christopher's neck and shoulder were right there. He licked them and his teeth extended. It would be so easy to mark Christopher as his, but he had to wait. They needed to do that together, mate to mate. That was something he wanted to be freely given, not taken.

"Fredrik," Christopher groaned.

Never had he expected just hearing his name could be so erotic. There was no stream of dirty talk or explanations of what Christopher was going to do to him. Just his own name sent ripples running through him. Christopher hadn't even moved. His patience alone was almost enough to drive him out of his mind.

"Move," he whispered. "I…."

Christopher slowly flicked his hips, just enough to drag his cock over the spot inside that made Fredrik's eyes cross and his vision blur.

Fredrik's breathing became shallow and panting. He wanted more, needed more, and Christopher seemed intent on denying him. "I need…."

Christopher leaned over him, gazing at him so intently, Fredrik was tempted to look away, the eye contact so powerful, it was nearly overwhelming. "Look at me. I know what you want. I need it too. This is us, you and me. It will never feel like this with anyone else… for either of us… forever."

"You know how to drive me crazy," Fredrik said accusingly.

"I know exactly what will make you feel good and how to heighten your pleasure. It's part of being my mate." Christopher smiled and slowly withdrew, then slid back into him at just the right angle.

Fredrik growled deep in his throat, his wolf happy beyond belief. Just when Fredrik was wondering if he could take any more, Christopher picked up his pace. After his earlier climax, Fredrik wasn't sure how quickly he could be ready for round two, but that wasn't a problem in the least. He was already throbbing, and the need to come was almost as great as it had been earlier. "I want…."

"I know. But you're going to have to hold off for me just a little." Christopher gripped Fredrik's cock, holding it still, flexing his fist every now and then, keeping Fredrik on the edge. He seemed to know exactly what Fredrik wanted and nearly gave it to him. It was exquisite torture.

Fredrik didn't know how much more he could take. His head already throbbed, and his body seemed strung tighter than a guitar string. He needed release badly, but Christopher seemed determined to see how long he could make Fredrik wait. "Christopher… please."

"Not yet. Soon, I promise, but not quite yet." He pressed deeper and thrust faster. Fredrik hoped that signaled that Christopher was as close as he was.

Fredrik couldn't think clearly and held on to the bedding, letting his mate take him for the ride of his life. Within seconds he could take no more. Christopher seemed to sense it as well and began stroking him slowly. After being held on the edge for so long, it was more than enough, and Fredrik came in a rush that left him with sparkles behind his vision as he gasped for air. Christopher climaxed right behind him, and Fredrik wished he had seen him, but his eyes had already closed from near-complete exhaustion.

Neither of them moved for a long while. Fredrik was already tired, his energy reserves drying up quickly. When Christopher pulled away, climbing off the bed, all Fredrik wanted to do was roll onto his side. But he knew if he did, he'd be asleep in seconds, so he stayed still. When Christopher returned, Fredrik started when a wet cloth slid over his belly.

"It's all right. Just keep your eyes closed and let yourself float away."

"Uh-huh," Fredrik breathed.

Christopher dried him and pulled up the covers. Fredrik was instantly warm enough, completely content. He remembered Christopher getting into bed and a light kiss on the shoulder. After that, there was nothing as he fell into a deep sleep, the energy that had been swirling in his head back where it belonged—for the time being, at least.

THE FOLLOWING morning, Christopher ended up on the bottom of a pile of pups out in the grass. Snarls, yips, wagging tails, and excitement surrounded him as they all jumped and crawled over him in his gray wolf form. Nate and Pietro had asked if they could be wolfies after breakfast, and Christopher had agreed to play with them. He'd helped them shift before leading the parade outside. Of course, others had joined in, and Fredrik hadn't been able to stop himself from watching his sleek mate play with the young ones.

Fredrik eventually turned away and went in search of Stephan. He found him working on the new cabin under Jerry's leadership, making repairs from the storm damage. "What can I do?" Fredrik asked.

"We lost a few shingles, and one of the windows will need to be repaired, but otherwise it came through pretty well. Once the repairs are done, we'll get started inside. How about you go inside and clean up what was tossed in to keep it from blowing around?"

"I can do that," Fredrik agreed and opened the door. He carried out the scraps and set them near the fire area where they could be burned one evening.

When he returned, Stephan was working on the window near the door.

"I need some information that you might know," Fredrik said.

Stephan stopped removing pieces of the broken windowpane. "I'll try."

"Are you aware of the death of anyone in my family recently? We found two pups with the hunters a few days ago. I know they're related to me because of their eyes, but I don't know how, or why Juneau would have anything to do with the people who took the pups. It's all very strange."

"I don't think anyone has died or been killed recently. There hadn't been any recent challenges before I left."

"Dang it," Fredrik swore.

"Well, I pretty much tried to stay out of family business, if you know what I mean. That sort of thing can get you killed. If you get in good with one part of the family, then you're a target of another faction. It was ugly."

"Tell me about it." Fredrik huffed. "I know these pups are related to me somehow. As I said, the eyes are a dead giveaway. But I need to know where they came from. If they're my nephews, I need to see if I can get them back to their mother."

Stephan shook his head and turned back to his work.

"What?"

"If you don't mind me saying, it doesn't matter. The pups are better off here than they are with anyone in your family. They'll have a chance at a proper childhood, and they'll be loved. There's no love in your family. It's all about power and position. Having pups is only a way to move up in the family ranks, especially if you breed strong ones that could be leaders."

Fredrik wished he knew of a way to find out without actually contacting anyone in the family. If his mother were still alive, she'd know. She'd kept tabs on all of them for self-preservation purposes.

He went back inside to go to work.

"There was Anatolia," Stephan said. "I remember her being one of the few good ones."

"Yeah. She was." Fredrik remembered his cousin's smiling face from when they were kids. In the end, as she got older, she had been driven nearly crazy. "She ran away." Not that he blamed her. She was always wonderful, and her sweet nature had made her even more of a target.

"Yes, she did," Stephan agreed. "Could she have had pups?"

Fredrik felt cold. He supposed it was possible. But if Pietro and Nate were her pups, what had happened to her? "It's possible, I suppose." He could ask the boys what their mother's name was and hope they knew enough to be able to tell him. He hadn't wanted to ask them because it might have been painful, but he didn't have much choice. "She left four years ago." Could she have been pregnant at the time? Maybe she'd gone to keep her children away from their family.

Stephan returned to his work, and so did Fredrik. He hoped to hell Anatolia was still alive. If she was, losing her pups must have been more painful than Fredrik could imagine. He had to find out somehow. And if she was alive, he needed to find her. If she wasn't, then he needed to know what had happened to her. Of all his family members, only she was worth the effort to find out.

"Hey," Christopher said as he approached, and Fredrik humphed when each leg was buffeted by a playfully snarling pup. "You're a deer. Just so you know."

"I am, huh?" He smiled and lifted Pietro into his arms. Nate bumped his leg, and Christopher lifted him as well. "I have some work to do here. I can't be a deer right now."

They both looked heartbroken until Christopher's mother came out with food. Then they forgot all about it and raced over, little tails flying out behind them.

"I'll get them dressed," Christopher said. "Mom said she'd watch them so we could get some work done. I think she's thrilled to be a grandmother again, even if it may be temporary."

Fredrik nodded. "I think they could be my cousin's boys, but I'm not sure. We're going to have to talk to both of them and see what they can tell us." He was not looking forward to that conversation one bit.

"You knew you couldn't put it off for very long."

"I know."

Christopher took the boys to get them to shift so he could dress them. "Wolfie time is over for now," he told them as he took them to the cabin.

112

"Wolfie time," Stephan said, chuckling. "Where have I heard that term before?" He met Fredrik's gaze, and Fredrik knew. Anatolia used to say something like that when they were kids. They had to be her boys. He hadn't remembered until that moment. He used to be a wolfie when they played together.

Fredrik sighed and went back to work. There was no one he could ask about her. His family would be no help, and he wasn't going to approach them anyway. Staying out of his brother's way and not drawing his attention was the best method he had for keeping trouble at bay.

Christopher returned with both boys dressed and tugging at their shirts.

"Where are their shoes?"

"That was the compromise we made in order to get them to keep their clothes on," Christopher explained. "Now, do you want to see Grandma?" he asked the boys.

"Yes," they answered quietly, clearly not liking the clothes they were wearing.

"We wanna be wolfies," Pietro explained.

"You can be wolfies after a while. You need to eat lunch, and then you can spend some time with Grandma," Fredrik said gently.

"Okay." Food and Grandma seemed to stop the argument.

"Thank you," Fredrik said, kneeling down to hug both of them. "I'll be up to eat soon, and once I'm done with my work, we'll both be wolfies with you."

They nodded, and Christopher took them to the pack house.

Fredrik watched them go and then got back to work, keeping his mind on the task at hand. Of course, after he returned, Christopher kept distracting him, first by pulling off his shirt, which Fredrik wasn't sure he was happy about. Letting everyone else ogle his mate was something his wolf didn't like. And then, when Christopher got to work, his scent intensified, and Fredrik had to try to keep upwind so he could think with something other than his dick.

When he got hungry, he took a break and found the boys inside, crashed out on one of the sofas.

"The poor dears are exhausted," Christopher's mother said.

"I know," Fredrik said. "I need to talk to them about their mother, but I'm not sure how to do it."

Christopher's mother nodded gently. "If you're asking my advice, I'd say just ask them what you want to know in the simplest terms possible, and don't be surprised if they can't or won't answer. They may not have the words for what they're feeling or want to say, so be patient. They've been through a lot."

"I know, and I'm trying to figure out just how much."

"If you're gentle and patient, you may find out more than you want to know."

He knew that was a distinct possibility, given the fear they'd displayed at raised voices and the way they'd cowered during the storm. He knew if he made a sharp noise, they'd be awake and near panic in seconds. "I'll do my best." He sat, and she brought him a plate.

Christopher had followed him in and took the seat next to his, sharing a smile and leaning close enough to bump shoulders. They ate without much conversation so the boys could rest. Once they were done, they both thanked Christopher's mother and then left the house and the sleeping pups, returning to work.

Later that afternoon, as Fredrik was getting ready for a break, he stepped outside, covered in dust, and was nearly barreled over by the two little wolfies. Fredrik stripped and shifted, watching as Christopher did the same. Soon the four of them were rolling around on the soft grass away from the building site. The boys needed to learn to hunt and stalk, so they played games that would help them as they got older. Christopher taught them to play pounce, but the only one who seemed to do the pouncing was Christopher, and always on Fredrik. It really wasn't fair—not that he was complaining.

It was a good afternoon, and it got better when the pups settled down and the four of them curled up in the grass. Fredrik rested his head on Christopher's shoulder, his wolf licking his mate as they lazed in the shade. The pups, of course, were the first to get their energy back, nipping at their ears and tails, pouncing on their backs after trying to sneak up on them.

Fredrik batted Nate away and scolded him with a growl when his bite got too intense. The pup rolled over, showing his belly to say he knew he'd been bad. Part of Fredrik wanted to find his cousin so he would know she was all right and to return her pups to her, but another part hated the thought of letting the pups go. Christopher seemed to understand his dilemma and gently licked the side of his muzzle. Fredrik huffed, put his head back down on his mate, and tried not to think about it.

CHAPTER 6

EVERYTHING HAD been quiet for the past three days—no more storms, attacks, or people or wolves scouting around the compound. Mikael had sent Christopher out on regular patrols to see that their land was marked and that there weren't any additional encroachments. Christopher also helped with the removal of the bodies of the hunters off pack land. He'd gone back to check on them just yesterday, and the scavengers and carrion feeders had done a remarkable job of scattering what was left of them. In a few days, they would join the list of people who went into the backwoods areas and never returned. If anything were found, it would look like they had been attacked by wild animals, which in a way they had.

"Why so preoccupied?" Mikael asked as Christopher crossed the compound to get to work on the cabin, which was coming along nicely.

Christopher shrugged. "I keep thinking about Fredrik. He's my mate, and I'll do anything I can for him…."

"But now it's him and two pups?" Mikael inquired, and Christopher nodded.

"They're great kids, but I never thought I'd be a father, and I certainly didn't think it would happen a few days after meeting my mate." His thoughts had spun for days, and he'd tried to get a handle on them, but he had been so busy with working on the cabin, patrols, and then making time for Fredrik and the pups that he hadn't had any time. He wondered if that was how most parents survived, on no sleep and with no time to think about what they were doing.

"The gifts the Mother gives us happen in her time, not ours. We need to be grateful. No one said that finding your mate was going to be easy, and even after you do, life isn't a picnic."

"It seems like that for you and Denton," Christopher groused childishly.

Mikael chuckled, and Christopher's temper rose. "If you'd been here when Denton and I met, you wouldn't say so. He made me work for it, make no mistake about that, and I'm so glad I did. He was worth it, and I think if you look at things objectively, you'll realize that Fredrik is worth it too."

"Of course he is!"

"Then stop complaining and whining about your lot in life and make the most of it." He stalked closer, power radiating off him. "Denton and I would give our eyeteeth to have those boys. He would make an amazing father, and I would love to have pups. But we never will, because I would never allow anyone to touch my mate, not even for the purpose of having pups, and the thought of his scent in someone else is more than my wolf would allow. Denton feels the same way." He raised his lip slightly, flashing a hint of teeth to show just how serious he was. "I could decree that Denton and I would raise Nate and Pietro. I'd never do that, but I could. And I was tempted to." The anger in his expression slipped away.

"You don't know what it's like…."

"What what's like?" Karl asked as he joined them.

"Little brother here is having a pity party," Mikael said with little heat.

"Actually, I was trying to ask some advice from my alpha. But that didn't go so well." Christopher met Mikael's eyes and didn't back down, even when Mikael growled.

"That's enough, you two," Karl scolded and turned to Mikael. "You need to remember that Christopher is an adult member of the pack and deserves to be treated that way. And you…," Karl said, turning to Christopher. "Being an alpha is about taking care of the entire pack. That's a lot of responsibility, so being a help instead of a pain in the ass is always appreciated."

Mikael nodded, and Karl looked at both of them in turn, then walked away.

"Dang," Christopher said.

"So what did you want to talk to me about?" Mikael asked.

"The storm," Christopher said. "There are some things I don't understand."

"I'll help if I can," Mikael said, and Christopher realized just the kind of man his brother truly was. He didn't pretend to have all the answers.

"It's about Fredrik. I've been meaning to ask, but things have been busy. Umm, the storm wasn't natural. I think you know that."

"Yeah. There was something dark in it."

"Yeah. Well, Fredrik told me he's been hearing voices. That a woman has been talking to him. He said it happened in the cave, as well as before that, and then again the night of the storm. He said that she told him that she needed his help. That there was only so much she could do." Christopher gulped. "I watched him rush out during the storm, and it seemed like he was communicating with it, maybe making it move. He said he sent it back where it came from and then the power in it broke. Then he was so tired, I had to carry him indoors, and he went right to sleep."

"You said he heard the voice in the cave."

"Yeah." Christopher had a pretty good idea what it could mean, but he wasn't sure. "I thought that since that was the domain of the Mother, maybe…."

"Yes, it may have been her trying to use Fredrik to help protect us."

"He said afterward that he'd let something inside him out of its box and couldn't put it back. But after… later… you know…." He hated stammering, but talking to his brother about sex seemed… yucky… as the pups said when he tried to make them eat peas.

"I get the picture, and that doesn't surprise me. You're his mate. If there is something inside him that's hard for him to control, then you might have the other piece he needs to control it."

"But what could it be?"

Mikael gestured toward the deck and led the way up, then sat in one of the chairs. Christopher sat next to him. "The Mother told me before I met Denton that Anton was not of the light. That he wasn't one of her children. I thought all wolves were. But he was a dark wolf, and Fredrik has some of that in him. You can see it in the color of his eyes. The dark wolves have powers because some of them sell their souls to get it, and that gets passed on to their children. I think it's part of the bargain."

"But Fredrik…. He's so not like that."

"No, he isn't. He had someone in his life to show him love. That is their ultimate undoing. They don't really care about one another, only about power and how to get more of it. Anton was strong. He bullied, harassed, murdered, burned, and raped his way to the top, and he planned to stay there."

"But the storm…."

"It was born of darkness, so darkness was needed to defeat it. The Mother said she wasn't able to, but Fredrik could." Mikael sighed. "I don't claim to understand the Mother or how everything in that realm works. A lot of what I know comes from studying the old stories. But I would guess that if the Mother asked for Fredrik's help, then he has to be powerful."

"That's what I was afraid of."

"He's your mate. You will never have anything to fear from him. He will protect you above everyone else, and he would sell his soul before he allowed any harm to come to you or those boys. That's what matehood and family truly mean."

"But what if I can't help him control it?" Christopher asked.

Mikael leaned forward, meeting his gaze with a full-on alpha stare. "That's the heart of this, isn't it? You're afraid you can't be there for him. That you might not be good enough."

Fuck, it hurt to hear Mikael say that, but he had to admit he was dead-on. Christopher swallowed and nodded slowly.

"You are his mate," Mikael said in measured tones. "That means you are enough for him, and that the same things he'd do for you, you would do for him, without hesitation and without doubt. It isn't always easy. Having a mate isn't always perfect, and you won't always get along, but your mate completes you." Mikael shifted a little nervously in his chair. "I'm not always the easiest person the live with. I can be distant and short, especially when I'm working and everything is flowing. An interruption is the last thing I want."

"I remember."

"I wondered for a while after Denton came here if I wasn't needed so much anymore. Because I could work through the day without being interrupted. It took me a while to realize that Denton was running interference. He took care of the smaller issues and held what was more important until I was done. If it was a true emergency, he interrupted me... in a very interesting way... that I won't go into."

Christopher smiled when Mikael blushed slightly.

"He knows me better than anyone, and he's made me a better leader because he's what I need and I'm what he needs. Apart, we were good alphas, but together, we're unbeatable. So if you want my advice, it's to worry less about whether you're good enough and learn to value what you have."

"Okay." Christopher stood. "I appreciate you listening."

"That's a big part of what I do. Now if I could just get the other packs to listen. I was really hoping they would come together more quickly than they have. Some are fine and getting stronger, but others seem to be floundering."

"Maybe the storm the other day isn't the only way darkness can be spread."

Mikael nodded. "I've thought of that, and it's possible. Most of what's going on is just the packs finding equilibrium once again. Some have had two leaders already. I expect I'll have to step in eventually, but I keep hoping they'll work things out for themselves."

"Well, thanks." He was glad he wasn't part of that struggle. He had hated his brother for a while after he'd told him he wasn't going to get the pack he wanted to lead. Now he saw his brother was right. The responsibility was too much. Hell, he was worried about a mate and two pups. That was hardly an entire pack.

"Anytime," Mikael said. When Christopher began to walk away, Mikael stopped him. "I've given some thought to what you said a few days ago, and I have an idea. Jerry makes most of the furniture that we use. He's very talented. I was thinking that once we have the cabin done, maybe we could get a group of interested pack members together to help Jerry make some furniture and other items that we could sell. I want you to work with him to develop ideas and places we can sell them. We are growing and need more sources of income."

Christopher grinned. "You mean it?"

"Yeah, I do. I also want to talk about where the pack is spending its money and how we can make the most of it."

Christopher nodded. "We grow some vegetables and things, but some of them don't do very well because they die if we get a cold snap. What if we only grow what does well and then take that to a market? We could sell our produce and buy other things that we need. We'd be better off, and we might be able to help some of the other packs that are struggling."

"Get your ideas on paper and think them through. We'll go over them in a few weeks. Don't rush. Make sure what you have is solid. This is the entire pack we're talking about, so we want to do things right."

"I will." Christopher hurried down the steps and over to the guest cabin. He burst inside and found it empty. He left once again and scented his mate. Christopher smelled his trail, but it was faint. He followed the scent, and it slowly got stronger. He started grinning widely when he realized where he was being led.

Christopher stripped at the edge of the forest, leaving his clothes in a pile, and shifted. His senses heightened, and he easily followed the scent, zipping over fallen logs and around huge trees that had seen his father and grandfather. As he approached the creek, he heard splashing and puppyish yips. When he stepped into the small clearing, he sat and watched as the pups splashed in the shallow water, Fredrik sitting nearby, watching them. He knew Fredrik was aware he was there; he could scent his excitement and hear his elevated heart rate. Eventually Christopher trotted over and sat next to Fredrik's magnificent black wolf, lightly licking his muzzle and then nuzzling under his mouth. In this form they couldn't talk, but communication was definitely possible. It was more basic and primitive, but in some ways clearer—their wolves communicating the most basic of feelings.

Fredrik turned to him, licking his neck, rough tongue smoothing his fur. He leaned against him slightly, scanning the area for any danger.

Christopher neither saw nor scented anything, and yipped slightly. The pups looked up from whatever game they were playing and then crouched low in the grass, tails up, waving from side to side as they inched forward, stalking their prey. Christopher would have laughed if he were in human form, but instead he pounced when Pietro did, catching him in midair and rolling him down to the ground. Nate pounced next, and Christopher did the same, yipping once again and then showing the pups how to hunt properly.

They imitated him as best they could and their technique improved some. Of course, after a while, they lost interest and wandered back to the water, chasing the tiny fish and splashing over the rocks.

Fredrik barked and growled a warning.

Instantly Christopher scented and scanned where Fredrik was watching. A wolf was out there. He sniffed again. It was definitely a shifter, in wolf form, with a sour smell that nearly made his stomach turn. The pups scented it as well, looked back at him, and then took off across the stream. Fredrik ran after them, and Christopher did the same. He caught up to Nate, grabbed him by the nape, and carried him back across the stream.

Fredrik joined him with Pietro, holding the pup as he watched the woods on the other side. They set the pups down, herding them together, protecting them as the smell got stronger. Finally a wolf stepped from the woods, blacker than Fredrik, smelling like he'd rolled in every dead thing for miles.

Christopher shifted to human form. "Who is that?" he asked Fredrik, who stared back at him, widening his wolf eyes. Christopher looked at the wolf. "Is that your brother?" Fredrik bobbed his head, and Christopher curled his lip in disgust. Then he reached into the stream, picked up a rock, and hurled it at the wolf. Juneau didn't move, and that was his mistake. It hit almost where Christopher was aiming, bouncing off his rear leg. Christopher picked up another without hesitating. "I can hit you with each shot. You move and I'll still bean you."

The wolf growled, baring a mouth full of huge teeth.

"Try it. The next one will be between your eyes, and if I get you down, I'll rip you apart without hesitation. Now get off pack land."

Fredrik sent up a howl that was sure to bring help, then returned Juneau's growl. Christopher expected the wolf to turn and leave, but he stepped back to the edge of the trees and then shifted into a huge man.

"You don't have what it takes to take me on," Juneau sneered.

"Try me. We took on the likes of you before, and look what happened. You lost everything."

"We lost because Anton became weak." Juneau curled his upper lip in disgust. "I won't make that same mistake."

"You already have. You have made more mistakes than you know." Christopher stood straight and tall, staring into deep, soulless black eyes. Fredrik's eyes were the same color, but they were full of life and energy; these were nothing like that. "The others are coming, so unless you want our entire pack coming down on you, I suggest you turn tail and run."

"I didn't come for you, pup. I came for him. He's from my pack, and I will have him back."

"No," Christopher said with a cocky smile. He was nervous as hell, but there was no way he was going to show it for a second. "Fredrik and the pups are mine. They belong here. Your mistake was messing with my pack."

"He killed one of my pack members. That will not go unanswered."

"You attacked and held one of mine. Fredrik brought back a loved member of our pack and did away with a pile of crap from yours. I'd say we were even and the world is better off."

123

The scent of other wolves coming up behind them carried on the breeze. Juneau had to smell them by now. Fredrik remained on guard over the pups as others broke into the clearing.

Juneau stood his ground, letting everyone gather, then shifted and slowly walked into the trees.

"Who was that?" Mikael demanded after he shifted.

"That was Fredrik's brother. I think he wanted to send a message, but he got more than he bargained for," Christopher answered.

Mikael turned to Catherine and Kaiawa, and they took off at full speed across the stream and into the woods. "I heard you." Mikael smiled. "You did good holding your own that way. Never showed weakness, even if you're intimidated or nervous. You projected strength."

"Thanks." Christopher shifted back into wolf form and joined Fredrik and the pups. He comforted Pietro and Nate with gentle licks and then did the same for his mate. They were his, all three of them, and come hell or high water, no one was going to take them away. The thought of Juneau coming close to any of them set his blood boiling, and he nearly snarled just from the memory.

Kaiawa and Catherine returned. For the first time, Christopher noticed Stephan was there, and then Stephan stepped forward, openly checking out Kaiawa. Christopher didn't know the stoic Native American wolf very well. He mostly kept to himself, but that was likely to change if what Christopher thought was true.

Mikael motioned back toward the pack compound, shifted, and gave a short bark before running into the woods. He went at full speed, as did the others, leaving Fredrik and Christopher to bring up the rear with the pups. They took their time, the pups sensing that something very serious was happening and following dutifully, though they still explored every nook and cranny along the way.

As they approached the compound, snarls and barks reached his ears. Christopher knew something was very wrong. A bark and then a growl tore the air, followed by a high-pitched cry of pain, a second, and then another. Christopher wanted to hurry to find out what was going on, but he stayed with Fredrik and the pups to protect them.

"Don't you dare show your sorry asses here again! Next time I'll skin you all alive and use your mangy hides for welcome mats." There was no escaping the rage in Mikael's voice.

Christopher cautiously stepped into the compound. It was a mess, with broken chairs and bits of hide and fur.

"They didn't get into any of the buildings," Mikael observed.

"I got everyone to the pack house," Karl said, grabbing some water and rinsing his mouth. "Damn, they tasted foul."

"How many were there?" Fredrik asked.

"Three. I think Juneau was acting as a distraction to get us away. Didn't work with Karl and the others here. He and Denton sent two of them limping away, and Catherine got her claws into a third on his way out. They won't come back here again. We're too powerful for them, and they know it."

Christopher agreed, but it was what Mikael didn't say that worried him. No, they wouldn't come here openly again, but that didn't mean they wouldn't try to lure pack members away or sneak in. They would try something, he was sure of that. He wished he knew what.

He retrieved his clothes and shifted, then dressed quickly. He got Fredrik and the pups inside and then went back out to help clean up the mess. It wasn't as bad as he'd originally thought. Most of the outdoor furniture had been overturned, with just a few pieces broken. Those they carried to Jerry's work area for him to repair when he had a chance.

When things were back to normal and the others had joined them from the pack house, Mikael and Denton went around to everyone, soothing them as best they could, while others went on patrol to make sure the encroachers were truly gone.

"Are you okay?" Christopher asked Fredrik as soon as he got inside the guest cabin. He wrapped his mate in his arms, and they sat on the sofa with the two pups. The pups refused to shift, not even for food, and the men comforted them with light strokes and soft caresses until they finally fell asleep.

"I hate that Juneau turned what should have been a fun outing into an afternoon of terrorism and intimidation. The pups deserve better than that, and so do you."

Christopher noticed Fredrik left himself out of that statement.

"It would be best if I put some distance between me, my brother, and your pack."

"Are we back to that?" Christopher whispered, but he might as well have been yelling with all the intensity behind it. "First thing, the pack all came to our aid—your aid—without a moment's thought, and second, do you really think that lunatic is going to let up on anything or anyone because you leave?" Christopher shook his head. "He isn't going to stop any more than your father did."

A knock sounded on the door, and Christopher quietly said to come in, knowing any wolf would hear without raising his voice. The door opened and Jane came in. Her outgoing personality had dulled somewhat since her return. Not that he could blame her, but he hoped it would return.

"I know we're supposed to ignore it when we overhear conversations," she began, and Christopher motioned to one of the chairs, but she sat on the floor, gently stroking Nate's dark coat. "I don't want you to leave," she told Fredrik.

"I think I have to. I want everyone here safe."

She shook her head. "I wouldn't be here without you. I know part of what he'd have done to me, and afterward I expect he'd either have killed me or held me somewhere until I'd had his pups." She shivered, and Nate whimpered and skittered closer to her. She lifted him into her arms, and he settled once again. "We all need you."

"No, you don't."

"Actually, we do," Christopher said, adding his voice to hers. "I need you, and so do the pups. None of us would last very long without you."

126

"Yes, you would. I'm not strong, and I'm not important. I never have been."

"Bullshit," Christopher said and then looked at Jane.

"Don't worry, I've heard worse. Remember, we're supposed to ignore what we hear, but the sound of Mom and Dad…." She shook. "Apparently dirty talk is their thing, and noise-canceling headphones only do so much."

Both he and Fredrik shivered and then laughed. "Anyway, the thing is, you *are* strong," Christopher said. "Look what you did with the storm. And as for being important, just look at the pups and me. You're the center of our world. Never forget that."

Fredrik didn't look like he was buying it. He got up and went into the kitchen. He got out a pan, and soon the scent of popcorn and butter filled the entire house. By the time Fredrik brought over the bowl, both boys were awake, following their noses. "You have to shift if you want some. Wolfie time is over for now," Fredrik said.

"Do we have to?" Pietro asked after shifting.

"Yes," Christopher said as Nate shifted as well. "Go on and get dressed."

They both made faces that showed just how much they liked that idea.

"Is mean Alpha Juneau gonna come here?" Pietro asked.

"No. He's going to stay back where he belongs. And if we see him again, Fredrik and I will protect you, just like we did today, but you can't run. You have to stay with us." Christopher took their hands, led them to the second bedroom, and dressed them in simple clothes.

Once he was done, they raced back out for popcorn. Nate climbed up onto Jane's lap, shoving popcorn into his mouth by the handful.

Christopher was remarkably content just being with them. "I miss television," he said after a few minutes. "I used to watch it when I was in school."

"Then get one," Fredrik said. "My father and Juneau never allowed them at all. If they had, pack members would start to think for themselves. I used to watch as well, and I think that's part of what helped convince me just how full of crap my family was."

"I'd like to watch television," Jane said. "Kaiawa has a small one in his room. He lets me watch it sometimes. I don't think Alpha Mikael and Alpha Denton have one."

"I'll ask him if he minds. I don't think he will." Christopher shared a look with Jane. "What does your mother think?"

Jane pulled a face. "She hates television. Dad wanted to get one, and Mom said it was unwolflike."

"That sounds like her." He grabbed some popcorn before it was all gone. The boys always ate like they were starving.

"Did Alpha Juneau ever hurt either of you?" Christopher asked Pietro as gently as he could.

Pietro and Nate both shook their heads. "He's scary," Pietro said. "Mama hated him. She said he was a poopyhead."

"She did not," Nate countered. "She said he was a shithead, and you know it."

"It's the same thing, and you said a naughty word," Pietro said, throwing the popcorn in his hand at his brother.

"No throwing things, and we shouldn't talk that way. But it's okay because he was just telling us what your mama said. What was your mama's name?"

They looked at him like he was crazy. "Mama," they answered in unison.

"Did she have a name, like you? What did other people call her?" He was trying not to make a big deal out of this, but he could tell Fredrik was anxious for answers. They had agreed to try to wait for the right time, and since the boys had brought her up, he thought this might be their chance.

"Auntie Tolie," Nate answered, looking at his brother, who nodded. "She went to sleep and never woke up." He turned to Jane and buried his face in her shoulder.

Fredrik set the bowl on the table and took him, comforting Nate even as tears ran down his face, and Christopher did the same with

Pietro. This was a major breakthrough for the boys, even if it was a sad one for both them and Fredrik.

"It's all right. I know you miss your mama," Fredrik said quietly. "I miss mine too, and it's okay. You have me and Christopher, Alpha Mikael and Alpha Denton, and Grandma, and Aunt Catherine and Uncle Karl, and Jane." Fredrik kept his voice soft.

Christopher rubbed Pietro's back and let him cry out his loss.

"I should go," Jane said and stood, and Fredrik did as well and carefully hugged her. "I really want you to stay," she said.

Fredrik didn't answer her, and Christopher figured it was time to have a real discussion with his mate about this whole leaving thing.

"You're welcome anytime," Christopher said as he kissed Jane's cheek. "I know it's been hard, after what happened. But don't let it stop you from being you." She nodded, but Christopher thought it was more automatic than real agreement. "I know you were afraid, and that the men who took you scared you. But if you let that fear run your life, then they win."

"You sound like Mom," Jane said.

"Believe it or not, sometimes your mother is right. No matter how much we don't want her to be. Everyone in the pack is here to support and protect you. Caution is one thing, but living in fear is quite another." Christopher had noticed she hadn't left the compound since she'd returned. She used to enjoy going into town on the pack shopping trips. Now she always stayed behind. "It may be too soon, but the longer you put off going back to normal, the less likely you are to ever be able to do it."

"But what if they're out there?"

"They aren't. Remember, one of them is gone, I saw to that," Fredrik said. "And we aren't saying you should go alone. See if Karl, Kaiawa, or your dad will take you. But go and try to get back some of what they took from you. You're way too pretty and special to hide away. Even if your mother and father would rather see you kept here until you're thirty."

She smiled, and Fredrik hugged her once again. "I'll think about it." She left the cabin, and they sat back down, still comforting the boys.

"Can we be wolfies again?" Pietro asked.

"I'd rather you stayed boys for now. You'll be able to be wolfies later," Christopher said gently.

Being in their wolf form, the boys didn't have to deal with the range of emotions they did when in their human forms. They could hide and in a way protect themselves from what had happened to them. As wolves, even pups, they could bite and claw. That gave them a small amount of power and control, something both seemed to crave. That left Christopher wondering exactly what had happened to them, or more importantly, what they'd witnessed. He knew they needed to deal with those memories, and putting it off wasn't going to help them much, but neither was pushing. *Baby steps*, he kept telling himself. They needed to take baby steps; it was all the boys were capable of.

IT TOOK time, food, and lots of playing to wear the pups out and get them ready for bed. Neither of them wanted to sleep in their own room, but Fredrik was masterful at wearing them out to the point that they stopped arguing and simply fell asleep.

"They're becoming so important to me," Fredrik said as he undressed and got into bed.

Christopher knew they had to have a serious conversation, but his naked mate was almost enough to send his mind off on a completely different track. Heck, it was one that he desperately wanted to be on, and his wolf didn't give a crap about the stuff Christopher had to talk about. All he wanted was to be with his mate and make him his once more. "We need to talk." He purposely left on a pair of shorts or their conversation would never happen. "Every time things get tough or you get scared, you talk about leaving."

"It's for your own good."

"Like I'm going to buy that explanation. You can't bullshit a bullshitter, and I've played that game. I ran away from my pack because I couldn't see a place for myself, when all I really needed to do was be a part of the pack and a place magically opened for me... for both of us. So don't tell me it's for my own good. I know myself and what's best for me. Having you here is what I want and what's truly best for me and for the pups. So if you really want to go"—he pointed toward the front door—"then get out of the bed, pack your stuff, and go." He stared at Fredrik with the intensity of Medusa trying to stare at Perseus.

Fredrik didn't move, and his open mouth and wide eyes told Christopher that he hadn't been expecting that at all. "You're serious?"

"If you're going to fucking leave, then get on with it. If you're going to stay, then make up your mind and stick with it." He'd had it with this wishy-washyness, and it was time to put his cards on the table. He waited, but Fredrik didn't move. "Good. See? Making the right decision wasn't that fucking hard. You just go with your heart, and it always works."

"How did you get so wise all of a sudden?"

Christopher cringed slightly. "Mikael. That's what he told me in so many words. At least I think that was part of what he was trying to say. The making you choose was my idea." Lord knew what he would have done if Fredrik had actually gotten up to leave. His backup plan consisted of groveling. "As a pack, we're strong. If you and the pups want to be safe, then here is where you need to be."

"We could all leave," Fredrik suggested.

"No," he answered flatly. "All of us belong here. You, me, the pups. Hell, even the Mother is talking to you and asking for your help. So I take it to mean that she wants you to stay as well, and I doubt any of us could ask for a higher endorsement than that." He hoped he was right and lightning didn't come through the roof and strike him. He waited and breathed a sigh of relief.

Fredrik put up his hands. "All right. I give up. I'll stay." He grinned.

Christopher rolled his eyes. "Don't do us any favors. Stay because you want to stay." He moved closer to the bed, then turned around and slid his shorts down his legs to give Fredrik a view of his backside. "Stay because the thought of being without me for the rest of your life leaves a hole in your heart as big as the idea leaves in mine." He softened his voice and slowly turned around, giving Fredrik a full-on view of just how much he wanted him. Christopher's cock pointed straight at the ceiling, trying to climb to his belly button. He stalked closer, and it waved back and forth with each step, Fredrik's eyes following like he was watching a tennis match.

Fredrik's lips parted and he groaned softly. Christopher pulled the covers down on the bed, exposing his mate in all his rich-skinned glory, his cock throbbing and slapping his belly. Damn, he was gorgeous. Christopher lived in one of the most breathtakingly beautiful places on the planet, and he'd seen the natural wonders that surrounded him all his life, but nothing compared to Fredrik lying in his bed, waiting for him, eyes darker than the deep of night with wanton need.

He guided Fredrik onto his back, lying across the bed. Christopher took his cock in hand, pointing it at Fredrik's lips. Fredrik parted them, and Christopher slowly sank his cock between, watching as it disappeared into his mate's perfect mouth. He slowly rocked back and forth, in and out. Fredrik took all of him in, opening his throat so Christopher could disappear completely inside him. Damn, that was the most incredible sight ever. "God, baby, the things you do to me. You make me want things I don't know if I'll ever have the right to."

"You have me. All of me," Fredrik said when Christopher pulled back, and then, when he slipped between Fredrik's lips once more, Fredrik sucked him hard, pulling him deeper and deeper.

"I want all of you. I want you as my mate, always and forever," Christopher said. The thought of Fredrik leaving sent chills through him. He pushed that all from his mind and only thought about the fact that his mate had indeed chosen him. Christopher flexed his hips because he couldn't help himself. Fredrik's wet heat and pouty lips grabbing him, sliding along his cock, was too much for his wolf to bear. "Damn," he groaned.

Fredrik hummed and arched his back so he could take more of him. Then Fredrik reached for his arms and tugged him downward. At first Christopher resisted, but Fredrik tugged harder. Christopher leaned over him, hands on either side of his mate. Fredrik latched his hands onto Christopher's ass, pressing forward as Christopher sucked Fredrik's cock. He couldn't stop flexing his hips and was afraid to go too far.

"Fuck yeah." Frederik pulled off and swore when Christopher slid his lips down Fredrik's cock.

Christopher held him there, parting Fredrik's legs and running a finger over his opening. Fredrik quivered beneath him and began sucking on Christopher's cock once again. After a few minutes, Christopher let Fredrik's cock slip from between his lips, then lifted Fredrik's legs and buried his face between his firm cheeks. The scent of his mate was strongest there, and Christopher wanted more. He licked and sucked, thrusting his hips at the same time, the sensation of his mate surrounding him and the flavor of his mate on his tongue nearly sending him into erotic overdrive.

Christopher was nearly overcome with need. All he wanted was his mate. Everything that had gone on around them disappeared. There was no thought of Fredrik leaving, building cabins, or even psychotic brothers making threats. Even the rest of his pack and family receded as all his attention centered on his amazing mate. When Christopher quivered from excitement and he knew he could take no more, he pulled away from Fredrik and turned him on the bed.

Fredrik gasped as Christopher manhandled him onto the mattress and grabbed his ankles.

"I can't take any more," Christopher growled. "You have two seconds. Either run or I'm going to claim you as mine." He grabbed the lube from the bedside table and nearly spilled the contents everywhere as he fumbled the damn thing in his shaking hands. He squirted the slick on his hand and somehow managed to coat his cock without coming at that moment. He was razor-edge close and had to think unsexy thoughts, like his mother suddenly bursting into the room, to keep from spilling.

Christopher pressed into his mate, sighing loudly as tight, furnace-hot pressure surrounded him, pulling on his cock.

"Need!" Fredrik whimpered, rocking his head back and forth on the pillow. "You have to…."

"I know. Can't stop." He sank deeper, burying himself inside his mate, joining them body, heart, and soul. They were becoming one, and no one was going to tear them apart. He had found his mate, and Fredrik had agreed to be his. All that was required was the ultimate culmination: to bite and make it official and permanent for his wolf. Every cell in his body drove him forward. Instinct from deep inside his wolf came forward so fast and hard, there was no way his human half could control or stop it. Once he was buried deep, his wolf took over, driving into his mate, claiming Fredrik as Fredrik's own wolf came forward.

They didn't shift; it wasn't necessary. Their animal natures were in command, naturalistic power set on taking what his wolf already considered his, and he would not be denied. Words were replaced with growls and nips that Fredrik returned with equal enthusiasm. Christopher captured Fredrik's mouth, tugging on his lips, thrusting his tongue in to take possession. He needed all of Fredrik to be his, and thankfully his mate seemed more than willing to be taken.

Christopher plundered Fredrik's mouth as he pounded his incredibly lithe body. Nothing would ever be more perfect than this exact moment. He'd remember it always as that one where his body rose up, excitement building until he could take no more, his mate gasping, whimpering for him, gripping him tightly. His release was imminent. There was no holding back any longer. Christopher pulled from Fredrik's lips and licked a spot near the base of his neck, feeling the blood coursing through Fredrik, the source of his mate's life force. Parting his lips, he sank his extended teeth into his mate's flesh, taking some of that life force into himself, joining them together in a way that meant they could never be separated. As soon as the coppery taste of blood hit his tongue, the last of his control snapped and he came hard, marking Fredrik with his bite and adding his scent to Fredrik's.

Electricity zinged through him, and then warmth spread from deep inside all through his body, intensifying until he swore he was going to burn from the inside out. He pulled his mouth from Fredrik's neck and turned his face to the ceiling. He wanted to howl his joy at the top of his lungs, but Fredrik pulled him back down, kissing him, joining them together once again as his body convulsed beneath Christopher.

All went quiet after that. Christopher's mind was clearer than he could ever remember it being. Gone were the worries about matehood and whether he was good enough for Fredrik, or the doubts he'd had regarding the pups. They came with his mate, and he had accepted everything about his mate. Fredrik was his—that was all that mattered.

Christopher gathered Fredrik in his arms, holding him close. He wanted this moment to last forever, but, of course, nothing so wonderful could last long. The rush of endorphins faded, and their bodies separated in shudders and soft gasps. But even that wasn't like it was before. He could still feel his mate like a warmth in his chest that didn't fade or dull as the moments passed. "You're mine forever now. Can you feel it?"

"Yeah."

Christopher inhaled and grinned. "You smell different now, more like me. You still smell like you, but…."

"What?"

"It's hard to describe. Remember I said there was an undertone to your scent, earthy and yet acrid. Like your brother, only much less pronounced?" Christopher licked the mating bite, which was already looking less angry. He hated that Fredrik might have been hurt, even if it had been necessary to make their mating permanent. He inhaled again. "That part of your scent is gone, replaced by hints of me. Now that's really hot."

"You're such an animal," Fredrik teased.

"But I'm your animal, and don't you forget it." He bared his teeth, and Fredrik chuckled.

"You like that I smell like you."

"Damn right. You belong to me, and I want everyone to know it. If anyone from your family ever comes near you, I want them to know that you no longer belong to them. You are no longer a part of that world. You're part of my pack and belong in my life, not theirs."

"You know that will mean nothing to my brother."

"Mating bonds are sacred to all wolves. He cannot break them or change that, no matter what he does. Even the darkness knows that."

Fredrik went silent and didn't move, cocking his head to the side for a few seconds.

"You hear her, don't you?"

"Yes. She says you're right and that I am one of her children now." Fredrik closed his eyes, and Christopher rolled them on the bed so Fredrik rested on top of him. He continued holding him tight until Fredrik rested his head on Christopher's shoulder.

"Do you still feel that dark place inside you? The one you were so worried about after the storm?"

"Yes. It's still there. I don't think that will ever go away."

"Are you sure it's darkness?"

Fredrik lifted his head, staring into Christopher's eyes. "Of course it is. That's what my mother always told me. She said I shouldn't use it or I'd end up like my brother and father."

"What if she was wrong?" Christopher said.

He felt tension instantly rise in Fredrik. "She lived with them for years. She should know."

Christopher stroked up and down Fredrik's back, needing to comfort him and knowing how to settle him once again without being told. "I'm saying that our mating removed that part of your scent that was dark, so why would it stay inside you? What if what you thought was darkness wasn't?"

"Then what is it?"

"Power," Christopher said. "Mikael told me that your father was able to bring darkness to start a fire that burned along the old Evergreen pack lands, and we believe your brother added the darkness to the storm that you were able to shift away. So you have power of some sort. What if that power isn't dark or light? Maybe it just is, and your mother said not to use it because your father only used it for darkness."

"Huh."

"Our talents are gifts and nothing more. How we use them is up to us. Your father and brother used them to bring hurt, and that took over their souls, making them black and setting them outside the light. But you chose to set that aside. You saved Jane and brought her back. You also used your power to turn the storm away from those who care for you and turned it back on those that would hurt us."

"Okay."

A thought occurred to him that chilled Christopher to the core. "What if your brother realized it was you who pushed the storm back? What if he knows how much power is inside you because you bested him? What would he do?"

Fredrik shivered. "He'd try to make me use that power to further his interests." The shaking intensified. "And he'd come to me to try to see for himself. Maybe that was why he showed himself, so he could get a close look at me or maybe even smell me."

"But you smelled the same until we mated."

"Maybe there was something he didn't realize was there until he knew to scent for it. I don't know. But my brother doesn't do anything unless it has a purpose, and his purposes always benefit him." Fredrik rolled off Christopher and sat on the bed. "Maybe this was truly a mistake. You would all be safer if you were away from me."

"We are not going back to that," Christopher said firmly. "You are my mate, the only one I'm ever going to have. You know we mate for life, and separating would relegate both of us to a half life of loneliness and wishing for the other."

"Then what the hell do we do?"

"For one thing, I protect you along with the rest of the pack, and secondly, we work with you to discover just what this power is so you can learn to control it."

"I'll never use it again."

"Maybe not. But ignorance isn't bliss, no matter what some people may think. Not knowing what you have can be just as dangerous as your brother. If you understand what this power is and learn to control and use it when you want and in ways that are under your control, then you are better off, and that's all I care about."

"I don't know if I can. There is no one who understands anything about my power."

"Yes, there is… and she's been speaking to you." Christopher nodded to emphasize his point. "I suggest that tomorrow we ask Mikael and Denton to take us to the cave. Mikael says it's the closest place we have to the Mother, and I think we need to ask her for whatever she is willing to tell us."

Fredrik paled slightly. "I don't know if I want to."

"Why? If the Mother has already been talking to you, then she knows you and what's in your heart. I'm sure Mikael would tell you that if you weren't worthy, she wouldn't have anything to do with you." Christopher thought a minute. "Mikael is the only other person I've ever known the Mother to talk to directly. She has ways of making her wishes known, but direct communication is rare."

"What if it isn't her?"

"Then we'll see." Christopher held Fredrik and tried to soothe him. "You won't be alone. I can promise you that. So don't worry about it."

"How can I not?"

"Just remember who you are and what you've done. You're one of the strongest people I know."

"I am not."

"Says the man who killed a man to rescue someone he didn't know," Christopher countered. "Now just close your eyes and go to sleep." He lightly stroked up and down Fredrik's arm. "I could try to wear you out some more." The idea had his cock stirring almost instantly.

Fredrik groaned softly, as if he was considering it. "How about we both go to sleep? We can do that tomorrow after we've done this cave thing. It will give me something to look forward to."

Christopher hummed and closed his eyes, doing his best to calm Fredrik as fatigue crept in and he fell asleep cradling his mate.

"ARE YOU sure you need to do this?" Mikael asked both of them. Fredrik shrugged as Christopher nodded. "Which is it?" Mikael looked at each of them individually.

"I don't know if this is a good idea or not," Fredrik explained.

"The Mother is good, and I believe the worst that would happen is silence. We can ask questions of her, but the Mother decides what she'll answer and how she wishes to do it," Mikael explained.

"I think I have to know what this is inside me. My mother said it was the darkness, some of what was in my father. Christopher thinks it's a gift and that it isn't dark or light. I don't know who to believe."

"All right," Mikael said, getting up from his chair. Denton, who had been standing next to him, moved closer to flank his mate. "We'll go to the cave. But I want the two of you to go down to the creek and wash. Make sure you're clean and then shift and enter the cave. Denton and I will follow behind you."

"Okay," Christopher said, wondering what the ritual was for.

"When you're going to ask something of someone, you should make sure they understand that you're serious, and the first part of that is to look your best."

"Should we shift?"

"No. Stay in wolf form. It's the way we are closest to her. The Mother is the embodiment of the earth, wind, sky, sun, and all living things. So in our wolf form, we are closest to her, and it's easier for her to make her thoughts and wishes known to us."

Denton nodded his agreement. "You should go. We want to do this when the sun is at its height. That's when the Mother is at her most powerful."

"All right," Christopher said. "We'll make sure Mom can watch the pups, and then we'll go."

Mikael became very quiet. "No. Take them with you." Christopher was about to ask why but stopped. Mikael had a very faraway look in his eyes that snapped back to the present all of a sudden. "It's just a feeling," he said without further explanation.

"All right," Fredrik agreed, and Christopher followed him out of the pack house and over to the guest cabin.

"Can we be wolfies?" Pietro asked, running naked across the living room, with his brother right behind him.

"Boys, you need to dress," Christopher's mother said with failing patience.

"Yes, you can be wolfies. We need to go to the creek to take a wolfie bath and then we have somewhere important to go. You have to promise to be good and not to run around or fidget while we're there," Fredrik explained.

"Okay," Nate said and shifted into wolf form, with Pietro doing the same.

"Thanks, Mom," Christopher said and hugged her. She left right away, looking like she needed a rest. The boys sat on the floor, little tails going like crazy. He told them to stay where they were, and then he and Fredrik went into the bedroom, stripped and folded their clothes, and then shifted before rejoining the boys, who were getting fidgety. Christopher pushed open the door, and they stepped outside.

The pups barked softly, the wolfie version of "thank you," and then the four of them traipsed off into the woods toward the creek.

The pups loved the water, but today they were subdued, as if they realized something important was about to happen. They rolled in the moving water, shaking themselves into fluffballs, and then did it again. Fredrik helped Pietro, and Christopher made sure

Nate was clean everywhere, licking behind his ears at a spot he'd missed. Without being told, the pups got out and stood on the bank as Christopher helped Fredrik bathe, rubbing his side and stroking Fredrik's muzzle with his own. God, he loved the scent of his mate, and when they were clean, he shook and then rubbed Fredrik once again, making sure his mate carried his scent and he carried Fredrik's. Then and only then did he slowly lead them down the creek and up to the cave entrance.

Fredrik went inside, and the pups followed, with Christopher bringing up the rear. They sat on the stone floor, the pups' usual energy at bay as they looked around. Christopher sat next to Fredrik and gathered the pups next to them, and they waited.

Of course, the pups began to fidget, looking at each other and then up at them. Fredrik nudged them back into position when they tried to move away and lightly nipped at their backsides when they stood. They were so cute, and he was sure Fredrik would have liked to have been able to let them run and explore. Fredrik's nerves were definitely on edge, and Christopher figured he wanted everyone to behave.

Finally Denton and Mikael entered in their wolf forms, stepping regally to the raised stone platform. Mikael shifted and Denton followed, and then they pulled on white robes and stood together.

"The Mother of us all, these wolves have a question they believe only you can answer for them," Mikael said.

Christopher turned to Fredrik, who closed his eyes. The pups stood still except for their tails, which bobbed from side to side.

The cave got very quiet.

"Concentrate on what you want to know and send it out. The Mother is near. She can hear what you ask," Mikael said.

The leaves on the trees outside the cave rustled in a breeze that built and then entered the cave in a swirl of air. Christopher hoped that was a sign that the Mother had heard Fredrik's request.

"I am here," a voice that swirled around them said in a gentle tone. "When my children have need of me, I am here. What is it you seek?"

Christopher wasn't sure if he should fall to the ground. Mikael and Denton didn't, but they bowed their heads, so Christopher did the same. The pups had gone very still, even their tails coming to a stop.

"You wish to know what lies inside you?" she said. "I cannot answer that for you. The content of the heart of each of my children is something they must figure out for themselves. Yes, I asked you to use the strength you have inside, and this troubles you."

Fredrik tilted his head slightly and looked up toward the ceiling. Christopher followed his gaze, seeing nothing but stone.

"As has always been true, each one chooses his destiny. Yes, your mates are a gift that I can bestow on you, but the others come from the universe, and I cannot change them or guide you in their use. That must come from you, but I can say that you decide how you use your gifts. The decision you make will determine the course of your life, as well as that of your mate and the pups you have with you."

Fredrik made a gentle growling sound that sounded like he was trying to talk.

"Everything in your life is what you make it. Never forget that. All of you. Each of you has one life, and you must decide how you will live it. Nothing is written or decided for you, including how you use the gifts you are given. So choose wisely, all of you." The breeze came close, swirling around the pups, who jumped and tried to play with it.

Gentle laughter filled the room, and then the breeze swirled all around them one last time before the air suddenly stilled.

"I think that's all the answer you are going to get," Mikael said.

Fredrik extended his front paws, bowing low, and then nudged the pups toward the exit. Christopher bared his neck to his brother and Denton, waiting until they shifted before following them out into the sunshine and leading them all back to the compound. Fredrik didn't seem to be in a hurry, and his wolf looked lost in thought. When they reached the cabin, Fredrik went right inside with the boys, and soon Christopher heard whining about wanting more wolfie time.

"You need to get dressed, and then you can go out and play. But remember, you have to keep your clothes on, and no shifting unless you ask. I don't want wolves or naked children running around the compound."

Christopher stayed in wolf form, amused by Fredrik and the boys.

"Do you think Fredrik got what he needed?" Mikael asked as he stepped out of the woods. He shook his entire body like he was shaking water out of his fur.

Christopher wasn't sure what Fredrik got out of what the Mother had told him, but to him, she seemed to have confirmed that what was inside Fredrik was his to control and use. That the power was neither good nor bad, but the actions of the wielder determined its purpose. Not the other way around.

"Go on and shift," Mikael told him. "There's work to do, and I'm sure if you and Fredrik think about what was asked and what was said, the two of you will know the right path to take and how to use what she told you."

"BUT SHE didn't really tell me anything," Fredrik said after Christopher had dressed and was getting ready to help work on the cabin. He wanted it done so he could move them all into their permanent home. He also had some ideas for furniture making that he wanted to discuss with Jerry, but all that had to wait until this project was over.

"Yes, she did. Granted, I couldn't hear your questions, but her answers seemed clear. What's in your heart and how you decide to use the gifts you're given are what's important."

"Okay, I get that. But the power I feel still seems wrong somehow."

"Because you saw your father use his power to make others miserable and to bring hurt and pain. You aren't like that and you never will be."

"Don't be so sure—she said I had decisions to make and that they would affect all of us. It feels like a weight on my shoulders, because if I mess up, I could make us all miserable."

"You won't mess up. I know that. You'll do what's right and good because that's who you are. What I don't understand is how you can't see what everyone else can. Sure, we all make mistakes, but I doubt you're going to make a bad decision that's going to put all of us at risk."

"But she said so…."

Christopher was becoming frustrated. To his mind, the answer the Mother had given was crystal clear and the one that Fredrik seemed to have wanted. "Your destiny is your own, and your future—our future—will be based on the choices you and I make. Nothing is written in stone, just like you weren't born to be like your father. He made decisions that determined his path in life and his ultimate death. You'll do the same, and I'm betting your decisions will be much better than his."

"I wish I had your confidence. After that storm, it felt like there was so much swirling around in my head, and it all felt like it was so out of control."

"Maybe you need to work with whatever it is inside and figure out what you can do." Christopher stepped closer. "Once you know, maybe you'll feel better about it."

"I suppose you could be right. But if I'm going to let whatever this is loose, I need to do it away from the pack compound and not in front of the pups. I don't want them to be afraid of me."

"All right. I think I know where we can go. I'll take you there once I'm done with work."

"I don't want you there in case you get hurt."

"I'm not going to leave you alone. If you're going to figure out what's going on inside you, I'm going to be there for you." Christopher kissed him firmly to bring the conversation to a close, then said good-bye and left the cabin so he could get to work.

Christopher was coming to like hard labor. It cleared his head and helped him see what was important. The cabins themselves were fairly simple. They were wolves and didn't need a lot of fancy surroundings. The basics fit very well for them.

Today they worked inside. Christopher spent much of the day with Jerry in the kitchen area, getting the area prepped for the basic plumbing and the cabinets that were going to be installed. The plans called for a simple stove, refrigerator, a few cabinets for storage, and a sink for washing up. They wouldn't need much more than that since many of the meals were prepared by the other pack members and served in the pack house, or outside when the weather was good.

Denton and some other pack members were working in the bathroom. They'd had to go into town to purchase the supplies they needed, and Christopher worried sometimes that they were using too much of the pack's financial resources.

"What are you thinking?" Jerry asked, looking up from his measuring tape.

"Just that it would be good to get done. Mikael asked me to work with you to see if there were things we could build to sell. All the furniture in the cabin is rustically beautiful, and we were thinking that we could put some pieces together, we might make some money."

"I'll have to think about that," Jerry said. "Though a lot of what I've made has been the same basic piece, just decorated a little differently. We could start with some tables and chairs and see how they sell."

"There's a market we could try selling at and see how it goes, but I'll need a number of pieces to start. Maybe three tables with four chairs each. Something like that."

"I'll look into it and see what I can come up with." Jerry returned to work, and Christopher watched and helped as best he could.

"Christopher, can you help in here a minute?" Denton called, and Jerry motioned for him to go. Working on the outside, he'd been able to help because a lot of the tasks were repetitive, but inside, they seemed to require more skill than he had, so he mainly helped the others get their tasks done. Still, he kept himself busy until hunger took over and they all stopped for the night.

Fredrik met him outside with the pups each holding a hand. Damn, he was adorable like that. Pietro tugged at the collar of his shirt with his free hand, and Nate squirmed like his clothes itched. Christopher remembered being young and not understanding why he couldn't be in wolf form all the time. "Your sister is going to watch the boys for us," Fredrik said.

"Auntie Cathy is scary," Nate said before putting his thumb in his mouth.

Fredrik gently pulled it out. "Auntie Cathy isn't scary. She's just strong."

"She yells," Pietro said.

"Auntie Cathy growls because she's a wolf, and if you're good, what does Auntie Cathy give you?" Christopher knew his sister was strong and could be intimidating, but she was also warm and kind to the people who mattered, and that was what he wanted the boys to remember.

"Ice cream," Nate answered, shuffling from foot to foot like he needed to go to the bathroom. Christopher lifted him into his arms and took him inside, let him use the potty, and then carried him to where Fredrik waited for them outside Catherine and Stan's cabin.

"I hear you're mean and scary," Christopher said to his sister when she opened the door.

Catherine growled and bared her teeth before breaking into a smile and lifting Pietro into her arms, spinning him around until he squealed with glee.

"I want a turn," Nate said.

It seemed that scary Auntie Cathy had been forgotten.

"You guys do what you need to. I'll watch these two hooligans while you're gone."

Damn, he loved his sister sometimes. He also wished he could fully understand her. She could be gruff, caring, sweet, kind, and hard as hell all within the span of three minutes.

"Thank you," Christopher said, and Fredrik thanked her as well. They shared a quick hug, which was rather surprising, and he tamped down a flash of jealousy before leading Fredrik out of the compound and into the trees.

"Where are we going?"

"To the far side of the creek. There's a clearing there. It's near the very edge of our lands and should be remote enough that you won't have to worry about anything."

"Okay. But I don't even understand what I need to do. The Mother told me how to move the storm, and I did what she said. I don't want to create a storm, and there isn't one to move, so I'm not sure what I should do."

"You'll figure it out." Christopher tried to smile, but Fredrik didn't seem convinced.

CHAPTER 7

"Is THAT the best you've got? *You'll figure it out?*" Fredrik stopped and stared at his mate, wanting to smack him on the side of his head. "That's the best advice you can come up with?"

"I don't know."

"Of course you don't. Your head isn't filled with crap you don't understand, and it isn't you who's afraid as shit of what might happen if I release whatever this power is inside me. Maybe it's best if I just hold it in and forget about it."

"Is that what you really think?"

"How in the hell do I know? We asked the Mother, and she was little help. Some answers would have been nice, since she used me to do something she couldn't." Fredrik sighed. "Maybe I should try to find one of my sisters or a cousin who isn't a complete shit and see if they know anything."

"No!" Christopher said. "I don't want you going anywhere near any of them. What if they're in league with your brother?" He grabbed Fredrik's arm and tugged him close, wrapping him in his strong arms. "I don't want you to put yourself in danger. Let's see what you can do on your own, okay? Those people are scary."

"I know, but they may have the answers I need," Fredrik said as they resumed their walk.

"We're almost there," Christopher said, taking his hand and leading him through a thicket of trees and brush until they stepped into a break in the lush canopy. "What can I do to help?"

Fredrik shrugged. He really had no idea what he was supposed to do. "Nothing." He let go of Christopher's hand and walked to the center of the clearing, the grass nearly up to his knees. Once he was there, he looked up toward the clear sky and then concentrated inward, opening the box deep inside where he'd always kept what he'd thought of as his dark side.

He didn't feel any different. There was nothing at all. Fredrik turned to Christopher, shrugging, and then turned his gaze skyward once more, hoping something would come to him. Nothing did. He felt no different.

"Try thinking how you did during the storm," Christopher said.

He'd tried reaching out then, but there had been the storm and something to react with. Right now he felt kind of dumb standing in the middle of a clearing with nothing to do and no idea if anything would happen if he tried.

"What do you want?" Christopher asked as he approached. "What did you see your father do?"

Fredrik shivered. "I won't act like that."

"I'm not saying to do anything bad, but I think he started a fire and then directed it toward the old Evergreen pack compound. At least that's what Mikael and Denton think happened." Christopher hurried back to the trees and hauled a log to the center of the clearing. "See if you can set that on fire."

"I can't, I know that."

"Okay. You could move a storm. See if you can make the wind blow."

This whole thing was stupid. He knew he couldn't control the wind, but he closed his eyes and tried to concentrate. Of course, nothing happened, not even a breeze, and he wasn't fucking surprised. "Maybe we should go back to the compound. I don't know what this is supposed to achieve."

"During the storm, you were able to fight whatever was in it and then move it away and back on the person controlling it. I'm assuming it was your brother, but…."

"I don't know, but it felt like Juneau to me. I had something to work against, and I was angry and fearful for the pack."

"Do you think that's what did it?"

149

"I don't know." Fredrik's frustration grew by the second. "I was able to do what I did because I had no other choice. But I can't conjure up a storm just so I can move it around at will to see what I can do. It doesn't seem to work that way."

"What did it feel like?" Christopher asked.

"Like I could see inside the storm and feel its energy. Because I could do that, I was able to affect that energy and use that to move it away from me. There's nothing like that here, just birds and trees and a deer right over there. See? No storm or blackness intent on threatening us."

"So the power you felt and what seemed out of control at that time...."

"Is gone and yet it's not gone. I know it's still there, but I can't get to it." Fredrik began walking back the way they came. "I wish I had a better explanation for you, but I don't. I can still feel it there, but it's just out of reach. My head is calm and quiet, and there are no swirls of energy threatening to overwhelm me if I don't carefully keep them under control. It's always been like that."

"Maybe it only comes out when you need it," Christopher offered.

He shook his head. That wasn't it either, but he didn't know how to explain it. "When I released it before, I thought I'd never get the genie back in the bottle, and now I'm not sure if I'll ever be able to access it again."

"This power must come from somewhere."

"What do you mean? It comes from me."

"I don't think so. I mean, we're shifters, and I suppose being able to change forms requires some sort of special internal force that allows us to do what humans can't. I don't want to say magic, but some sort of energy we feel naturally that humans can't. So maybe the power you have is like that. It comes from somewhere outside, and then you channel it." Christopher stumbled over his words as his speech got faster. "We aren't strong enough ourselves to control or manipulate a storm, so the power must come from somewhere."

"So what are you saying?" Fredrik asked, wishing Christopher would come to the point.

"Can you try following the power to its source?"

Fredrik nodded and closed his eyes once again, concentrating on the slow vibration that always seemed to be there. It felt like an ever-present hum in the background of his mind, always there, rarely changing. As he thought harder, the hum increased, the pitch becoming higher and faster. "I can feel it." Slowly he pulled, and the tingling power became more pronounced. It was right there, just out of his grasp, and yet he had some control. He continued concentrating, nudging and tugging until it grew more forceful. His entire body thrummed with energy, just like it had in the storm, but now he had control and it wasn't threatening to overwhelm him—at least not yet. "What should I do with it?" Fredrik gritted his teeth as the intensity increased.

"Create a breeze," Christopher told him.

Fredrik directed the energy into the air, which moved and swirled around them. He opened his eyes and watched as the trees around the clearing swayed and danced in the breeze, and the grass waved as the air brushed over it. He was afraid to add more energy and put all his efforts into controlling what he was doing.

"That's awesome! Where is it coming from?"

"Everywhere." Fredrik smiled as patterns formed in his mind. Ribbons of shimmer flowed toward him and then swirled in arcs all around him, joining with the breeze he'd created, powering it, keeping the air moving. "This is amazing." Fredrik felt truly alive and somehow in tune with the universe, as though he was now part of its rhythm and melody. "It's like music." He increased the pitch, and the wind sped up, lifting leaves and pine needles from the forest floor. They circled and swayed, players in the symphony that rang in his head. He slowed the pitch and lowered the volume to that of a lullaby, and the wind turned into a light summer breeze, the debris tumbling gently back to earth. When he ended it, all was silent. Fredrik took a single step toward Christopher and tumbled to the ground.

"Fredrik!"

"I'm okay," he said, breathing deeply to let his head clear. "I was light-headed for a minute." He started to get back up, and Christopher was there, steadying him and insisting he sit for a while. "Wow, it was like I had all the power in the world at my fingertips, and as long as I used it, it sustained me, but as soon as I released it...." He shook his head. "It fed back on me and... wow."

"So it doesn't use your energy?" Christopher asked.

"No. But it's like it exacts a price when I'm done. I took and manipulated something from the universe, so it wanted something back from me." Fredrik went stock-still as a realization slammed into him. "That's the source."

"Excuse me?" Christopher said, still holding his arm.

Fredrick turned to him, his mind racing as ideas broke over him. "My father used this power all the time. It was how he became strong, but using it has a price. Checks and balances. I bet the more he used it, the more it fed on him, so the more he used it to try to compensate and remain strong and powerful. Over time it ate at his soul and...."

"It became an addiction."

"Yeah. I bet my brother is the same way. He desperately wants power and to feel and be stronger than anyone else."

"You used the power to defeat his storm."

"Yes. And I believe he knows that. Why else would he suddenly show up alone to check me out? I'm stronger than he is, and he's aware of it, so he's going to either try to eliminate me...."

"Or control you," Christopher supplied as Fredrik felt him shake and then step away. He twirled in a slow circle. "We need to get out of here, now. There are multiple wolves a short distance away, and they aren't our pack." Christopher helped him back toward the trees, and they moved as quickly as they could.

"I don't smell them." Fredrik realized that other than the heaviest scents, everything else was lost to him. The forest he'd always known seemed strange and somewhat alien, like parts of it had been ripped away. He continued breathing as they hurried between the trees.

"They're trying to flank us." Christopher changed direction and picked up the pace.

"Should we shift?"

"No time." Christopher led him down a path and then off it.

When Fredrik scented again, the undertones of the forest began to appear, and he could vaguely discern the other wolves, but direction was impossible to tell. He hated that he couldn't smell worth a damn and was relying on Christopher. Not that he didn't trust his mate, but two noses were better than one.

"This way," Christopher said. They changed directions again, circling a set of mammoth trees. Then Christopher took off through a small area where the trees seemed to part.

Fredrik could smell the scent of the prey that had used this area as a highway not long before. "How close are they?" he asked.

"Their flanking move didn't work. They weren't fast enough, but unfortunately we're upwind of them so I can't get a good read." He didn't stop but turned to him. "Why can't you smell them?"

"Wish I knew. Maybe the whole power-use thing messes with my nose." There would be plenty of time to figure that out later. For right now, they needed to get the hell back to the compound.

Fredrik heard the sound of running water a few minutes later. They crossed the creek and kept going. Christopher lifted his head to the sky and let loose a cry that carried over the land. It was answered quickly, then again a few seconds later by a group of wolves. Fredrik watched the trees, expecting to see their pursuers at any time, but none appeared.

Mikael was the first to burst into the clearing. He scented and took off across the creek with Catherine, Karl, Kaiawa, and a few others right behind him. Denton stopped and Christopher explained what happened. Then Denton took off, bounding into the trees after the rest of the pack.

"Thank goodness for the cavalry," Fredrik said.

"This has got to end." Christopher spat, glaring in the direction of where they'd all gone. "These incursions onto our land have to stop."

Fredrik couldn't agree more, but that meant either Juneau's death or his own. There was little middle ground. Fredrik thought maybe if he were under his brother's control, he might be allowed to live, but that wasn't an option. If he couldn't be with Christopher, he might as well be dead. The thought of losing his magnificent mate, who put him above everything else, was more than he could bear. There was only one choice as far as he could see. Somehow he had to kill Juneau.

"We should get back in case this is another of those diversions," Christopher said.

Fredrik nodded his agreement, and they hurried through the woods toward the compound. Thankfully, all was quiet. Everyone was on guard, but there was no attack.

The pups hurried up to them as soon as they broke through the trees, and Fredrik caught Nate, lifting him into his arms and hugging him tight. Sometimes it shocked him how full and warm his heart became when the four of them were together. Christopher swung Pietro into the air, and the little boy squealed his delight as Christopher zoomed him to where all the others stood, watching the woods, ready for a fight.

Silence reigned for quite a while. Every ear was tuned for the smallest sound, the latest word from their alpha and pack mates. The tension thickened by the second, and mates worried and fidgeted. Poor Stan stood with his pups, trying not to look worried even as his eyes betrayed the depth of his concern.

A deep, rumbling howl echoed over the woods: the cry of victory. Fredrik turned to Christopher for confirmation that it was Mikael. He nodded, and then another cry rose, this one filled with anguish, which was joined by others, all hanging over the trees in a verbal pall. Every face paled at the same time as the pack members wondered who had been injured or worse. Every single wolf was family, and the group filtered up to the pack house deck, gathering closer together to support whoever was going to feel the loss the greatest.

Tension built and curled around all of them, lashing them together with invisible ropes of worry. Soon every eye was trained on a single spot as footsteps sounded just beyond the trees. Mikael emerged in human form, carrying a wolf in his arms. Instantly Fredrik recognized him as Kaiawa, and Stephan cried out and nearly fell down the stairs in a rush to get to him.

Mikael set the wolf gently on the ground. "He's alive but too weak to shift."

"Let me through," Christopher's mother called as she parted the crowd and hurried down the steps. They all gathered around Kaiawa as she knelt next to him and began issuing orders. "I need water and something clean to bandage him with. We have to stop the bleeding to give him a chance." A huge gash ran from the top of Kaiawa's leg to his belly. It was a miracle he hadn't bled out completely.

Fredrik could see there was no hope. Kaiawa's chest rose and fell slowly, and Fredrik could hear his heartbeat slowing. It pounded a faltering rhythm in his ears. There wasn't much time, no matter what he did.

Christopher moved closer, still holding Pietro, while Fredrik cradled a whimpering Nate. He didn't want the pups to see this, but he couldn't turn away.

Instantly, the humming inside Fredrik increased. He wasn't sure why, but energy swirled inside him. Unlike in the clearing, this energy had the same kind of heat he'd experienced during the storm. He put Nate on the ground and was on his way to Kaiawa before he could think.

"I need room to work," Christopher's mother scolded, but Fredrik ignored her and placed both of his hands on Kaiawa's coat. Stephan lightly cradled Kaiawa's neck.

Fredrik ignored all of them, closed his eyes, and concentrated. His hands warmed, and then heat spread through him. He thought about the lines of energy from the clearing, and when they appeared, instead of sending them into the air, he directed them into Kaiawa. How he knew to do that was a mystery, but he followed the instinct.

The others jerked away, and he heard them cry out in surprise. Fredrik wasn't sure if this would help or hurt, but it was too late now. Suddenly he was floating and everything and everyone fell away except him and Kaiawa. The energy kept flowing, and he was certain now that he was doing good. Kaiawa's heartbeat sounded in his ears like a metronome, getting stronger and faster by the second. But when he looked around, he didn't see anything familiar.

The world was gone, and they were surrounded by a sea of white. He wondered if they had both died. "Where are we?"

In the light.

"How do I get back?"

You have to find your own way, Fredrik.

"How?"

You brought yourself here and you must find your own way back. There is only so much I can do for you and Kaiawa. But I can tell you that you must follow your heart.

"I'm not sure I can." Instantly, firm hands settled on his shoulder. At first he thought they might have been hers, but the touch was familiar, safe, and he followed it, letting that touch bring him back.

When the scenery changed around him, he was once again kneeling on the grass. The heat was gone from his hands, and he did his best not to fall over. Stephan's soft sobs reached his ears, and Fredrik was sure he'd failed. He was afraid to look.

"You did it," Christopher whispered into his ear.

Kaiawa moved under his hands, and Fredrik pulled them away, watching as Kaiawa slowly got to his feet and then shifted.

Stephan pressed Fredrik out of the way so he could get to Kaiawa, his tears changing to those of celebration and joy.

"I'm okay, Pup," Kaiawa said in a softly rough voice. "I was in a very strange place for a while, but I'm back with you." Kaiawa turned to Fredrik. "Do you know where we were?"

"I think we were in the light. We were with her." A tingle went up his spine. "I think we were in her actual presence. She spoke to me, but it wasn't like before." Fredrik turned to Christopher. "She always sounded and felt like she was far away, but this time she was very close, and her words so much more… immediate." He got to his feet.

"Do you feel like you did earlier?"

"No," Fredrik said with a touch of shock. "I feel like I've slept for hours and that I can do anything." He scooped up Pietro and whirled him in a circle. Then he set him down and twirled Nate in turn.

"What did you do? And how did you know to do that?" Mikael asked him.

"I wish I knew. It was instinct. I just acted because I knew he was dying," Fredrik explained.

"Thank you," Kaiawa said. "I don't exactly know where we went, but I know it was you who took us there and brought us back."

"Yes, thank you," Stephan said, gratitude shining in his warm amber eyes. "I don't know what I'd have done if you didn't bring him back."

"You're both welcome. Now get Kaiawa inside so he can rest." Nearly dying and then getting healed had to have taken a lot out of him. Fredrik was beginning to feel tired as well, and he took the boys back to the guest cabin. Christopher joined him a few minutes later, and Fredrik left Nate and Pietro with him and went to lie down in the bedroom. He fell asleep almost instantly.

He woke as warmth slid in behind him, curling right up to his back and butt, nestling right in, making him warm. "Where are the boys?"

"In bed. They're sound asleep."

Fredrik hummed and closed his eyes. Everyone seemed to be where they should be, and he didn't need to worry any longer. Christopher slid an arm around him and rubbed his belly in lazy circles that had him humming and groaning like there was no tomorrow. He was excited and too damn tired to do anything about it, but dang, he needed Christopher something fierce.

"It's okay. I've got you." Christopher slid that roving hand farther down, encircling his cock, stroking just right, and damn, that touch felt awesome. He felt a bit like a schlump for not helping

Christopher out, but he just didn't have it in him. Christopher gripped him a little tighter, stroking with one hand and sliding the other arm around his neck, working his nipple between those magic fingers.

Fredrik stretched out to give Christopher better access, closing his eyes and riding the waves like a surfer, except this was a better rush and a more amazing ride than anyone ever got on any wave. "Oh yeah, right there," he moaned when Christopher moved the head of his cock with a little twisty motion that got everything going.

"I know what you want, and I'm gonna give it to you. Just lie back."

Fredrik did what those whispered words told him, easing back against Christopher and letting him have it all. He shivered and groaned, stretching and angling his hips just a little, taking what Christopher was giving, pressing inside Fredrik until his eyes crossed, his balls pulled tight, and that tingling started at the base of his back. Fuck, he loved that feeling, and Christopher went deep, touching him just right, holding him there for a long time, sending zings and shakes through him, backing away for only a few seconds, and then doing it again.

By the time Christopher was done, Fredrik was a bundle of fractured nerves and quaking need. He so desperately wanted to come, and yet he didn't want this to end. Christopher stroked just a little faster, twisting his hand ever so slightly.

Fredrik's vision doubled, and he gasped softly as the pressure became too great. "Chris…," he whined, clamping his eyes closed as his release overtook him and he came in a rush. Endorphins zinged through him, and he floated once more. Only this time he knew exactly where he was—with Christopher, his mate, in their bed.

"Better, honey?" Christopher asked.

"Oh, yeah," Fredrik breathed.

Christopher might have gotten something to clean him up, or in some part of his mind that he wasn't sure he believed, Christopher might have rolled him onto his back and licked him

158

clean. Either way, he was happy as hell, content, and quickly slipped back to sleep.

"EVERYONE," MIKAEL said, pacing the front of the assemblage in the main room of the pack house. At the moment he was acting more like a cat than a wolf. "I'm open to suggestions as to how we stop this."

"You could challenge Juneau and kill him the way you did his father," Jerry suggested.

Fredrik saw Denton's expression harden. That obviously wasn't a popular suggestion with him.

"What other choice do we have? They obviously don't respect our borders and have made continual incursions into our territory. They are intent on harassing us, and that cannot go unanswered," Karl said.

"What if we give them a taste of their own medicine? I know where Juneau lives. We could plan a visit to his territory," Stephan said. "He will only understand strength and plenty of it."

"I like that idea," Karl said. "Sometimes the best defense is a good offense, and we need to let him know there will be a price for messing with this pack."

Mikael nodded, clearly intrigued by the idea.

"Bringing some hurt to my brother will only be minimally effective unless he feels it directly." Fredrik stood. "If you decide to do this, then you have to know that he's selfish, so wounding his pride is only going to make him angrier. He's going to need to feel personal and direct pain, something to make him think twice before tangling with this pack again."

"What can you tell us about Juneau?" Mikael asked. "You are a member of this pack, but if you feel some lingering family loyalty, we'll respect that."

Fredrik shook his head. "That ended a long time ago. Juneau longs for things to be like they were under my father. The territories my father controlled have reverted back to independent packs, and he wants to change that. But the thing is, Juneau isn't my father. He's meaner, but not as smart. So he's all bite and muscle, with little to back them up." Fredrik turned to the rest of the pack. "But don't underestimate him. He can be as vicious as anyone I've ever met, and he shows no mercy to anyone for any reason."

"What's his weakness?"

"His ego," Fredrik answered Mikael. "He feels it's his right to pick up where my father left off. Like I said, he isn't that smart, but he thinks he's brilliant." Fredrik held Christopher's hand. "He also believes in fighting any way he can. There are no rules with him, and nothing is off the table." He felt drained and leaned against Christopher. He didn't like the idea of anyone in the pack coming near his brother. Juneau was unpredictable and unstable. He was also capable of causing great pain if he got his hands on anyone in the pack. Fredrik agreed something had to be done, but he hated that the pack was going to suffer because of him.

"All right, then. Are there any other suggestions?" Mikael asked. "Good."

"So are we going to plan something like we did with the hunters?" Catherine said.

"No. This time we'll do a better job than we did then." Mikael turned to Stephan and Fredrik. "I need a list of all the wolves in Juneau's compound. I want to know how big they are and their strengths and weaknesses. Also, any wolves that you think aren't truly loyal to him and might stay out of it. We have to know what we're going up against so we can think about what we want to accomplish."

"Yes, Alpha," Stephan said, and Fredrik agreed silently.

"Very good. I'll also need a layout of the compound so we can determine any blind or hidden spots that we can use and where Juneau and his men might hide. I don't want to put anyone at risk unnecessarily."

Everyone nodded.

"Get me everything by the end of the day so we can work up a plan. After that, we'll discuss it and see if we can improve it. Any questions?"

"Are we going to want to go in as wolves or humans?" Stan asked.

"I don't know yet. We'll have to see what information we have and what we need to do. But I'm thinking that Juneau's father tried to burn us out, so maybe we need to return the favor. Destroy everything and make it harder for him to do anything in the future. If he has to rebuild or find a new place to live, then he'd be too busy to bother any of us. But I'll finalize my ideas once we have the information we need."

That seemed to answer all the questions, so they broke up the meeting, and Christopher's mother and Anna brought out food as the pups joined them. Unlike many of the pack gatherings, this one had a somberness to it that even the pups felt. It probably should have. After all, they had been discussing going to war, and that should never be taken lightly.

"What do you think?" Christopher asked as he brought over two plates.

"I'm scared to death for everyone. We almost lost Kaiawa yesterday, and I don't want to see anyone else get hurt, especially you." The thought of anything happening to Christopher chilled him to the bone. "I know it's unavoidable, but I still don't like it."

"Come and eat. We're going to patrol the pack borders tonight to make sure we don't have any visitors."

"I suspected so."

"And Mikael will make sure we plan anything we're going to do. That way any danger will be minimized."

Fredrik nodded, but he found it impossible to describe just how much danger there was. Everyone in Juneau's sphere of influence lived in a constant state of fear, both of one another and of him. There was no telling how any of them would react. He was sure some would run and hide while others would fight just to try to keep in Juneau's good graces afterward. He took the plate Christopher offered and tried not to think too hard about it.

They went outside on the deck and found a place to sit, the pups joining them, each carrying a plate that was precariously close to spilling, but in the end, they were obviously proud they had been able to get their own food. He was finding little things like that were important to them, and to him.

"Can we be wolfies after dinner?" Nate asked.

"If you like," Fredrik said gently, not about to deny them anything at the moment, just like he leaned against Christopher, soaking in his mate's care and affection. He was going to need all the warmth he could get later.

The boys were happy and dug into their food, using forks like big boys.

Fredrik was coming to adore his family more by the minute, and he needed to protect them—that was the most important thing. Nothing else mattered.

"Eat," Christopher whispered and lightly bumped his shoulder.

Fredrik nodded and slowly began to eat, pulling his mind off what he had to do and concentrating on the here and now.

Pack conversation swirled around him. Some were excited over what they felt was the coming battle. Others were more reserved, most likely having seen this type of thing before and knowing the outcome was never assured.

Once he and Christopher were done eating, Fredrik took care of the dishes and then joined the boys and Christopher near their cabin, where the boys had already shifted and were waiting for him.

"We thought we'd run a little. I told the boys they could try to catch a rabbit." Christopher smirked, knowing full well the pups would never down a rabbit, but then, maybe he had something planned for them.

Fredrik stripped out of his clothes and shifted, with Christopher following, then let Christopher take the lead while he brought up the rear as they launched the hunting expedition. It felt amazing to run with his mate, and the boys were so playful. The rabbits were perfectly safe that night, since neither pup seemed to be able to concentrate on anything for more than a few minutes. Still, it felt good to run, and it helped clear his head. At one point Fredrik raced past the pups to

Christopher and tackled him playfully, and the pups joined in, piling on Christopher in a wolfie jam pile.

He couldn't remember the last time his heart was light enough for him to actually play. He had had fun at times, more of them lately than he felt he deserved. But actual play had been very rare in his life, and to have Christopher care enough to go along and be the object of their game was pretty awesome.

As it got dark, Christopher woofed and led the way back to the compound. By the time they reached the cabin, the pups were pooped, yawning and dragging as they walked. Fredrik shifted and dressed, then carried the boys into their room, where he got them to shift and then dressed them for bed. They said good night to Christopher and went directly to sleep with little fuss.

"I never gave much thought to being a parent, and now I think I'd miss it if I weren't," Christopher said when Fredrik joined him in the living room. "I got you and them all at once. One large package, and I wouldn't change a thing. Well, maybe I'd remove your psychotic brother from the picture, but other than that…."

"I wouldn't change a thing either. I have a family for the first time since my mother died." That was the truth. He wouldn't change anything about Christopher and the pups, and he had to keep them safe. Fredrik opened all the windows, letting the breeze blow through, then sat on the sofa next to Christopher. He needed to be near him, to imprint his scent into his brain and take what he could get at this very moment.

"Is something wrong?" Christopher asked.

"No. Everything is very right." He was at peace with what he had to do. It was going to be the hardest thing he'd ever done, but he had to try to take care of the mess that was his family. If he told Christopher what he planned, Christopher would have a fit, and Fredrik would back down—he knew that—and this was too important to allow anyone to talk him out of. This entire situation was because of his family, so he had to be the one to clean it up.

After a while spent just scenting the night air and listening to the quiet sounds of night, Fredrik went to bed, and Christopher joined one of the pack patrols. Fredrik hated being in the bed alone, but he eventually fell asleep.

Hours later, Christopher returned, exhausted, and once he was sure he was asleep, Fredrik got out of the bed, dressed, and silently left the cabin. He walked to the edge of the trees, taking one last look at the cabin where the three people who meant more to him than anything in the world lay sleeping. Then he stepped into the woods and let the darkness surround him.

CHAPTER 8

CHRISTOPHER INSTANTLY knew something was very wrong. His dreams had snapped to a dark place, and he woke with a start, panting and nearly panicked without knowing why. The bed was empty, and Christopher listened, knowing instantly that Fredrik wasn't in the cabin. It was still dark, and within seconds, a vise grip clamped over his heart.

Fredrik was gone.

"Fuck," he growled and leaped out of bed. Racing outside, he easily followed Fredrik's scent to the trees.

"What is it?" Karl asked as he approached at a run.

"Fredrik's gone." Christopher didn't give a rat's ass that he was naked in front of his brother.

Karl hurried to Catherine's door, and Jane opened it within seconds. "Go watch the pups at Christopher's." He turned and pulled off his clothes, then shifted to wolf form.

Christopher shifted as well and plunged into the trees, knowing his brother would be right behind him. His paws pounded the loamy forest floor, but he barely felt it, giving his wolf free rein. All he wanted was to find his mate, right the hell now. The trail was easy to follow, and it didn't take very long to know exactly where Fredrik was heading. He paused and sniffed as Karl came up next to him. The scent was getting stronger, so they had gained a lot of ground on him, but they were approaching the edge of their territory, and if they didn't catch up to him before then, things were going to get dicey.

Christopher raced forward, putting on all the speed he dared. It was still dark, and even with his wolf senses, too much speed was dangerous. They crossed out of pack land but continued on without pausing. There was no way he was going to just let his mate go.

Anger warred with concern, and for right now, the concern was winning out, with the anger fueling his energy. Heartache swirled through him as well, but that would debilitate him, so he kept it at bay. He'd use whatever gave him energy and deal with the rest later.

"Well, look what we have here."

The voice barely reached his wolf ears, but Christopher turned on a dime, his hind legs almost flying out from under him. Beating the earth, he headed in that direction, claws ripping up the ground the same way he pictured them tearing into anyone who hurt his mate.

"Your brother is going to want to see you, but first I think you and I have a score to settle. I'm going to stripe that pretty face of yours for what you did to my brother, and then, when I have you on the ground, I'm going to give you what you so desperately want." The menace in the voice pulled Christopher forward.

"You mean Tweedledee? He was so easy to kill," Fredrik said.

Christopher slowed, and Karl nearly ran into him. The wind blew Fredrik's and the other wolf's scent in their direction, and Christopher had to stop his wolf from gagging on the stench.

"What makes you think you aren't going to be just as easy, Tweedle Dipshit?" Dang, Fredrik was fierce, and Christopher would have been proud of his mate if he wasn't so angry at him for leaving.

He turned to Karl, who nodded once, and then Christopher leaped forward, bursting from the trees to where Fredrik and the other wolf stood. He didn't think or stop, barreling into the foul-smelling man, tearing into him. There was no fucking way he'd let anyone touch his mate.

The guy tried to shift, Christopher could feel it, but Christopher was already ripping and tearing, using his claws and teeth to protect his mate. He went for the throat, ripping it out of the guy just as he completed his shift. The wolf still tried to come at him, but Christopher had done too much damage, and within seconds, all that was left was a mangled wolf body on the ground.

His wolf wanted to howl at the top of his lungs, but that would have to wait until they were back in pack territory. For now he sniffed his mate, making sure he was unhurt, and then shifted. "What the fuck do you think you were doing?" Christopher growled, pulling Fredrik to him as Karl emerged from the woods.

"We need to get the hell out of here," Karl said.

"It's way too late for that," a deep voice said from behind him, and Christopher turned, recognizing the scent of Fredrik's brother. Christopher turned back to where Karl had been standing but only saw empty space. "It seems I've caught two trespassers in my territory, and one of them killed one of my betas." He looked down at the bloody pulp, kicking the corpse with a dull thud. "Maybe you did me a favor. He was too stupid to live, but he and his brother had their uses. You, on the other hand, can be of great use to me." Juneau turned to Fredrik as a group of wolves, in human form, emerged from the trees. Two of them grabbed Christopher, yanking him away from Fredrik, who was grabbed by two others.

"Just let us go," Christopher said.

But all he got in reply was a deep laugh that curdled his spine. "No way. I'm going to hold you in chains, and if you're lucky, I'll only use a little silver in them, just enough to keep you docile, but not enough to do any permanent damage… at first." He turned back to Fredrik. "If you want your mate—" He sneered and bared his teeth. "—to remain pain-free, you'll do exactly what I tell you."

"Don't do anything," Christopher said, and he got a punch to the head for his trouble.

"My little fag brother will do exactly as I say." Juneau yanked Fredrik's head to the side to expose Christopher's mating mark. "He'll do anything to protect his mate, and that includes using his power for my purposes." Juneau rubbed the mark, his mark, and Christopher struggled against his captors. Fredrik was his and no one else's. Juneau ignored him and turned to Fredrik, who straightened his head and glared at his brother.

"I will not," Fredrik said levelly. "I came here for one purpose, to make sure my pack, mate, and pups were protected."

Juneau laughed. "Your pups. Anatolia's pups, you mean, and as soon as I'm done with you two, I'll be retrieving them and returning them to their family, where they'll be properly trained in our ways."

"You killed her," Fredrik whispered.

"Of course I did. Haven't you figured it out by now? No one leaves my pack. Not then, not now, not ever! And that includes your little friend Stephan."

"Why let the hunters have them?"

"They were the price for their cooperation," Juneau answered with a shrug, and Christopher saw red. "Now I'll get them back, the whole thing will have cost me nothing, and I'll have you."

Fredrik shook his head. "As I said, I came here to make sure they were safe, and I meant it. I challenge you for your place as pack alpha."

Juneau looked stunned and then turned his head to the sky and cackled—a deep, slightly deranged laugh. "You certainly are not."

"Yes, I am. I officially challenge you to a fight to the death. You and me, alone, anything goes." Fredrik didn't falter, and, damn, Christopher's heart swelled with pride even as his soul filled with abject fear. "Even you know the rules of a challenge. You must accept it or forfeit your position." Fredrik turned to the other wolves. "Will you follow an alpha who proves himself a coward?"

Christopher stilled, wondering just what Fredrik was up to. He saw Juneau become agitated and knew instantly he truly was a coward. As long as he was in charge and no one called him on his bullying, he was fine, but obviously no one had ever stood up to him. Juneau was huge and packed with muscle, but the fear in his eyes was unmistakable, even if it only lasted for a fraction of a second.

"I'll take your puny challenge and have you dispatched before you can take a break."

"Then release Christopher," Fredrik commanded. "You are honor-bound to fulfill the challenge you accepted, and so am

168

I. You have no call to hold him, and to do so also shows your cowardice. The challenge settles all, as you know. There can be nothing outside it."

Shit, so that was his game. Fredrik had done this for him.

The men released him, and Christopher turned to where Karl had been, hoping he had gone back for help. He was pretty sure they wouldn't get there in time, because events were quickly spinning out of control.

"The challenge will take place in thirty minutes, in wolf form."

Fredrik shook his head. "I already set the terms, and you accepted them."

Christopher went over and stood next to Fredrik. "What are you doing?"

"Keeping our pack safe."

"How do you figure that?" Christopher asked.

"If I lose, his ego will be assuaged, and he'll move on to something else. If I win, he's out of the picture permanently."

"If you win...," Christopher said, shaking. All he kept seeing in his mind's eye was his mate eviscerated on the ground, still, leaving him alone for the rest of his life. "He's...."

"And you're naked," Fredrik said possessively. "You need to find something to cover yourself."

Christopher chose to shift instead, but he kept a close eye on everyone around him. He didn't trust any of them, and he'd already proven he was a match for at least some of them. Of course, if they chose to attack all at once, there was only so much he could do, but breaking the rules of a challenge was something no wolf would do, not even one as dark and self-serving as Juneau.

"Let's get on with it," Juneau said. "I have things I need to do once I'm done ripping you apart, little brother." He led the way into the trees.

Fredrik followed, and Christopher stayed at his side, keeping watch on those behind them. They didn't have to go far before they entered a clearing. It was surrounded by tall trees, old, gnarled, and twisted beyond belief. Christopher chilled instantly. This was unlike any other place he'd ever been. It was like the very earth pulled all the warmth out of the air.

"This is the pack challenge circle," Fredrik explained.

He nodded and blinked, trying to see beyond the trees, but a dark pall had fallen over everything. There was no fire, and what little light reached them from the stars seemed to end before it reached the ground. Christopher had never seen a place so devoid of everything. Even the crickets and night creatures were silent.

"We'll do this here," Juneau said, clearly pleased he'd led them to this place.

Christopher saw Fredrik shiver and moved closer. His mate felt cold, and Christopher leaned against him to try to warm him, but it didn't seem to have any effect. He wanted to ask Fredrik what kind of place this was, but he wasn't able to in this form. Even when he'd been away at university or living in the cave to figure things out, he'd never felt so far away from his pack and everything familiar to him. This place seemed part of another world—one he didn't want to visit.

"This place is sacred to us and our kind," Juneau said loudly as other wolves gathered around the edges of the clearing. "We are wolves, creatures of the night. The moon and stars provide our light and the cover we need to hunt. Darkness is our ally and friend, how we survive and flourish." He was clearly playing to the crowd.

Christopher knew he was spouting a load of crap, but he was also gaining insight into how Fredrik's former pack lived. They were definitely not of the light, and whatever dark force they seemed to venerate was certainly present in this place. Christopher hated the idea of Fredrik fighting here. The thought of him fighting at all sent bile into his throat. Christopher wasn't sure how he was going to stand aside and watch while his mate was hurt.

"We are all clear on the rules," Juneau said, still grandstanding for his pack mates. "The fight ends when I kill my little traitorous brother and then take his mate." He glanced at him, and Christopher bared his teeth. There was no way in hell anyone was going to be taking him anywhere. Not alive. The pack would raise the pups, but if his mate died, he didn't intend to remain behind. They would both go to the Mother in her garden.

"Win or lose, all who wish to leave this cursed pack may freely do so," Fredrik said, shouting down Juneau. "I was raised in this unhappy and toxic atmosphere. I understand how oppressive this pack is. No one cares or looks out for anyone else."

"We must be strong," Juneau cried to the sky.

"Callous and mean is not strong. It's bullying," Fredrik countered. "Other packs are not like this. Members care about and help each other. That's what makes the pack strong. Other alphas aren't self-absorbed psychotic assholes the way the leaders here have been."

Christopher wondered why Fredrik was antagonizing Juneau. He hoped there was a reason other than just talk. Though Fredrik wasn't a boaster. If he had something to say, he was usually straightforward and spoke his mind. The more Christopher thought about it, the more he hoped Fredrik had some plan he was following.

"The little traitor knows nothing!"

"I know everything," Fredrik said. "My family is tainted with a lust for power. My father has it, Juneau has it, and I thought I had it. I don't. Juneau wishes only to glorify his pathetic self."

Christopher saw the veins on Juneau's neck throb as anger radiated from him in every direction.

"My brother is a traitor to his family." Spit flew from Juneau's mouth.

"My family, as pathetic as all of you are, is a traitor to me and to each other. My family is sick and needs to be cut away from the family of wolves like a cancer, and I intend to make the first cut." Fredrik stayed calm while Juneau nearly jumped out of his skin.

Juneau raised his hands to the sky, and the stars disappeared behind clouds that formed above the circle, swirling and churning.

Fredrik lifted his head, and Christopher watched with keen wolf eyes as the swirling turned more and more violent. Then, like a black arm, the cloud dipped toward where Fredrik stood.

Christopher closed his eyes, unable to watch what was about to happen to his mate. He expected a crash and braced himself against

171

the expected onslaught from the wind. But he heard nothing, and when he opened his eyes, the sky was clear. In the distance, a boom rolled over the land, followed by silence.

"You'll need to do better than that. Oh, and you should probably send someone back to your house to clean up what's left of it."

Christopher would have laughed if he wasn't in wolf form. Instead, he woofed to let his mate know he understood what he was doing.

"I defeated the storm you used and sent it back on you. I defeated you then, and I've done so once again."

"You can't defeat me in single combat," Juneau said, jumping into the air, shifting as he leaped toward Fredrik.

A single gust of wind raced across the clearing, slamming into Juneau, lifting him and then throwing him against a tree. "You're done, Juneau." Fredrik held him in place, plastered to the tree. "You may have inherited father's ambition and complete lack of anything positive, but I got his power."

"How?" Juneau gasped as Fredrik increased the power pressing on him.

Christopher saw Fredrik almost grow, becoming stronger, while at the same time, he smelled his mate's scent shift back closer to the scent he'd had when they first met. Only now the acrid scent was growing stronger, mixing with that of his mate and threatening to overtake him.

"Fredrik," Christopher said after shifting. "That's enough." In an instant he understood what the Mother had meant. "You don't need to do this." He hurried over, placing his hands on Fredrik's shoulders. "You've already won, and you never laid a hand on him."

"If I finish him, all this is over."

"No, if you finish him, you become like your father," Christopher said, concentrating on the mate scent that he loved, but it was becoming harder and harder as the stench grew and his mate, the one he loved, became more and more foul. Fredrik was still his mate, and he always would be, but now he understood Fredrik's mother. She had fallen in love with Fredrik's father before he'd become the beast. "I don't want to be like your mother."

The wind stopped and everything grew instantly silent. Fredrik stepped back, and they stood together, watching as Juneau slumped to the ground.

"Not enough courage to finish the job?" Juneau sneered as he tried to get to his feet.

"He has more courage than you'll ever have," Christopher said.

"Then why not finish me off?"

"Because I don't want to be like you," Fredrik said and turned to Christopher. "It's what she meant, isn't it? The power isn't good or bad, but it's what I do with it that matters."

"Yes," Christopher said, nuzzling close as the stain on Fredrik's scent slipped away. He smelled like Fredrik once again: fresh, clean, with hint of earth under musk and the scent of their forest home. "She said you'd have to make a choice."

Fredrik turned back to his brother. "There's no way I'd ever want to be like him."

Juneau got to his feet, a determined look on his face, but Fredrik met his gaze.

"Don't even think about it. If you attack me, all bets are off. I spared your life, now it's up to you what you do with it."

Juneau suddenly seemed very confused, like everything he'd had drilled into his head was somehow wrong. Granted, it was, but to have that kind of revelation had to shake the foundations of his life.

"Go back to what's left of your home," Fredrik said.

"I have nothing," Juneau said.

Fredrik walked toward his brother, and Christopher wanted to stop him. "You have your life, and you can decide how you want to live it. Yes, your pack is gone, and so is most of your family. No one will follow you any longer."

"So I have nothing," he repeated.

"Actually, you have the chance at everything." Fredrik turned away. Christopher knew what he meant and tugged Fredrik to him.

"Let's go home. We have the boys to look after, and I want to be there when they wake up in the morning."

Christopher shifted and walked with Fredrik as they stepped into the woods and began the journey home.

HE SHIFTED once he was inside the cabin and led Fredrik to the bedroom. Christopher was exhausted and ready to collapse. "Don't ever think about doing that again."

Fredrik turned, meeting his gaze straight on. "I did what I had to do. Juneau isn't going to be causing any more trouble. The pack is safe, and so are you and the boys."

Christopher got up from where he'd been sitting on the edge of the bed and moved to stand in front of Fredrik. "If you ever run away again or decide you're going to take on one of your psychotic relatives alone again, so help me, I will put you over my knee and paddle that cute little ass of yours until it's good and red."

Fredrik shivered.

"You like the thought of that?"

Fredrik didn't answer.

"Fine. Then I will stay away from you and—"

"That would punish you too," Fredrik pointed out.

Christopher growled deep in his throat. "I'm trying to make a point here, but you keep spoiling it. We're mates and we work through things together. You don't go off on your own and damn near get yourself killed. Nor do you challenge relatives who have taken the left turn to Crazytown."

"Okay."

"I'm really angry, and I want you to understand that isn't acceptable."

"Okay," Fredrik repeated, and this time the answer sank in. "No psychotic relatives or stops in Crazytown. I think I can manage that."

"Sometimes you're a real pain in the ass," Christopher chided.

"Actually," Fredrik said, sliding his hand along Christopher's cock, and damn if he didn't forget what he was going to say and the fact that he was supposed to be angry at that particular moment. "I think it's you who tends to be a pain in the ass."

"You know, you can do that all you want, but…." Christopher swallowed hard as Fredrik gripped him tighter and pressed him back down onto the mattress. Damn, his mouth forgot how to work. He moved his lips, but no sounds came out. Fuck, that felt good. More than good. "You know I'm still angry at you."

"Yeah." Fredrik released him and shucked his clothes, then pushed him onto his back on the bed, climbing on top of him. God, that view was amazing. "But I loved the way you came to my rescue."

"Of course I did. You're my mate."

"Am I only your mate?" Fredrik asked.

"No. You're everything," Christopher said. "You're the sun, moon, and stars all rolled into one. You're what I want to see when I go to bed, and the first thing I want to see and feel in the morning. You, Fredrik, are it for me. There won't be another for as long as I live. Wolves mate for life, and I was lucky enough not only to find my mate, but to fall head over heels in love with him. Watching you take on Juneau nearly gave me a heart attack. All I could think about was what I would do if something happened to you."

"But I was fine and I had a plan."

"What if he'd been stronger? What if he'd have charged you when you weren't ready? He could have eviscerated you, and it would have done the same to my heart. Anything that happens to you happens to me." Christopher pulled Fredrik down, holding him tightly, sex forgotten as he nearly panicked for the umpteenth time since he'd awakened to find Fredrik gone. "I love you, Fredrik." He slid his fingers through Fredrik's silky hair, kissing him as though his life depended upon it. "You hold my heart in your hands, so be careful with it."

Fredrik trembled in Christopher's arms. "I never thought of things that way. You're so strong and take care of all of us."

"We take care of each other."

Fredrik nodded slowly. "You hold my heart too." He took Christopher's hand and settled it on his chest. "I love you too, and leaving was the hardest decision I've ever had to make. But you, Nate, and Pietro had to be safe. That was all that mattered."

Christopher blinked a few times to stop his eyes from watering. "How safe do you think any of us would be if you were gone? Without you, none of us would be safe from loneliness. You fill our lives with joy and happiness. Just watching you with the pups is enough to show how amazing you are. They're so lucky to have found you…. We all are." There was no doubt in his heart at all.

"I think we found them, remember?"

"No. They found us. Those pups went through a lot, losing their mother, in essence given away to the hunters for Mother knows what, and coming to you."

"Us," Fredrik corrected. "They found us. Or maybe the Mother sent them to us. They are my family, after all, and they could have inherited the same kind of abilities that I have."

"Then who better to teach them how to use and control those abilities? You'll show them control, and we'll teach them not to be afraid of what they can do, but to use their power properly." Christopher tugged Fredrik closer.

"I believe that's the lesson my family never learned. They always wanted the power and to hell with anything else," Fredrik told him. "That's how they were all raised. My father cared for nothing else."

"Maybe they'll learn."

Fredrik shook his head. "They are incapable of learning." He sighed. "Don't think for a second that we've put an end to all this. Another of my relatives will come forward to take over the leadership of the family. It's how things work, and that isn't going to change. The lure of power is too great."

"Then what do we do?" Christopher asked. "Because I'm getting a little sick of all this. I want a quieter life, and I want to start building the pack business to make our life and everyone else's here easier. I want to be able to take the pups swimming and let them run without having to worry about an attack, and blessed Mother, I want to take you back to the meadow and make love to you out in the open, where the Mother can see and bless the love we have for each other."

Fredrik stilled and then smiled. "She's laughing."

"Huh?"

"Yeah, and she said to tell you that she already blesses our love and that she doesn't need to see it all the damn time. She says that's what she has rabbits for." Fredrik grinned.

"What did you just tell her? I know you said something because you look like the cat that ate the canary."

"I said that if she hadn't made doing the rabbit thing feel so dang good, then we wouldn't do it all the time. She just laughed again and then said to go back to what we were doing and not to worry about my family for a while. She has things under control for now."

"I wonder what that means," Christopher said.

"Hell if I know. Sometimes she talks to me. That doesn't mean we sit around chatting about movies and doing each other's hair." Fredrik rolled his eyes, and Christopher lightly swatted Fredrik's butt. "I don't know how she thinks and maybe she'll talk to you sometime. But hey, she did give us permission to go back to what we were doing, and I really think I like that idea." Fredrik wriggled his hips, and Christopher forgot about goddesses, insane relatives, and everything else for as long as Fredrik pressed to him, his smooth, hot body sending waves of heat and desire through him. When they came together, it stole Christopher's breath, and when they brought each other to the peaks of passion, Christopher held his lover, mate, partner, and friend in his arms and was grateful to the Mother for gifting him Fredrik.

Be happy.

And he was.

EPILOGUE

"CAN'T WE be wolfies?" Pietro whined as he pulled on the collar of his shirt.

Nate did the same thing while hopping from leg to leg in order to put his pants on all by himself. "Yeah. I want to be a wolfie," Nate said, adding his two cents and dropping his pants before racing through the cabin they'd moved into a few months earlier.

"Nate, Pietro," Mikael said in that alpha voice that was always obeyed. "You need to get dressed, just the way I told you."

Nate skidded to a stop and walked back to his pants, then pulled them on without further comment. Pietro stopped pulling at his collar and sat on the floor, pulling on his socks before carrying his shoes to where Fredrik sat.

"Thank you," Fredrik mouthed to Mikael and knelt down to fasten Pietro's shoes. "You need to behave so Alpha Mikael can do what we talked about last night. Do you remember?"

Nate nodded solemnly and then his lips drew up into a smile— something the boys did more and more.

The past few months had been blessedly quiet. Fredrik and Christopher had moved into their own cabin and had really begun building their permanent life together. The most traumatic thing had taken place the week after he had confronted his brother, when they found his body hanging just across their pack border. Fredrik wanted to think that Juneau had taken his own life, but he wasn't sure. Fredrik had dug a grave nearby and buried his brother, then said a short prayer, hoping he'd found some sort of peace. Other than that, he hadn't heard anything at all from his family.

"After that, we'll all run as wolves," Mikael said, and both boys accepted the explanation without question. There were many times Fredrik wished he were an alpha so the boys would always listen to him.

"Will everyone be there?" Pietro asked, suddenly standing straight and acting as grown up as his nearly four-year-old body would allow. He worshipped Alpha Mikael and thought the sun rose and set around him.

"Yes. This is something the entire pack, including all the pups, is included in. So get ready and act like big boys." He smiled at both of them, gently touching each of their heads as he turned his attention to Fredrik and Christopher. "We're leaving in fifteen minutes." He winked to let them know he'd stopped by just to make sure they were all set and to lend a hand if necessary.

Once Mikael left, the boys were easy to corral, and all four of them stepped outside and joined the rest of the pack in the compound.

Excitement bubbled in the chilly fall afternoon air. Fredrik was surprised Mikael's talk was still working, especially as leaves fell around them. Nate and Pietro had recently discovered the joy of "hunting" the colorful leaves as they fell.

Mikael raised himself to his full height, with Denton next to him. Nothing was said, but instantly every pack member grew quiet. He looked out over them and then turned, and the assembled group entered the woods. Fredrik knew they were going to the cave where they'd consulted the Mother a few months earlier. The whole pack, and that now included him, knew the way. What surprised him most was the solemn anticipation that came over the entire group. They walked in near-complete silence until they got to the creek.

He'd come to expect that everyone would enter the cave as wolves and then shift to their human form, and they all went through the process, finding their robes all laid out on the other side, even two small ones for Nate and Pietro.

They put on their robes and looked at each other, grinning and bouncing with excitement.

"Old Faithful pack," Mikael said as he stepped up on the rock ledge, "today is the autumnal equinox, and we take this day to honor the gift that Mother has given us, ask her help to see us through the winter, and most importantly, officially welcome new members into our pack family."

Denton motioned, and Stephan stepped forward and stood in front of Mikael. "Do you pledge your honor and loyalty to the Old Faithful pack, promising to defend and stand by your pack brothers and sisters?" Mikael asked him.

"I do."

Mikael looked up to the rest of the pack. "Do you accept Stephan into your pack family?"

"We do," they all answered in unison.

Mikael leaned forward, and Stephan bared his neck to show his deference to his new alpha. "Welcome to the Old Faithful family." Mikael smiled, and Stephan nodded and returned to his place next to Kaiawa, who held him close.

Fredrik took a minute to wonder what was up with them. They were quite obviously mates, but Stephan wasn't sporting a mating mark and neither was Kaiawa.

"Christopher, Fredrik, Nate, and Pietro," Denton called.

Fredrik herded the boys behind Christopher until they had taken their place.

"Fredrik, do you pledge your honor and loyalty to the Old Faithful pack, promising to defend and stand by your pack brothers and sisters?"

"I do."

"Fredrik and Christopher, do you pledge to be good parents to Pietro and Nate? To love, care, nurture, and protect them as though they were your biological pups?"

"We do," he and Christopher answered, gently pulling their pups closer.

"Pietro, do you promise to be a good pup and to listen to your daddy and papa?"

Pietro and Nate had decided that Fredrik would be Papa and Christopher would be Daddy.

"I do, Alpha Mikael. I love my daddy and papa."

Fredrik blinked and lifted Pietro into his arms, hiding the tears that welled.

"I do too," Nate said as Christopher lifted him. "I love Papa and Daddy too."

"Then I declare Nate, Pietro, Christopher, and Fredrik a family."

"Forever?" Pietro asked.

"Yes," Mikael answered him. "They're your papa and daddy for always."

Pietro put his arms around Fredrik's neck, and Fredrik found Christopher's hand as the four of them turned to face their pack.

A light breeze entered the cave, swirling around them. Fredrik felt what almost seemed like the light caress of a hand against his cheek. Christopher smiled and closed his eyes, and Fredrik knew he'd felt it too. Then the breeze died and the air became still once again. They had been blessed and were indeed a family, now and forever.

YELLOWSTONE WOLVES

CHALLENGE the DARKNESS

Dirk Greyson

Yellowstone Wolves: Book One

When alpha shifter Mikael Volokov is called to witness a challenge, he learns the evil and power-hungry Anton Gregor will stop at nothing to attain victory. Knowing he will need alliances to keep his pack together, Mikael requests a congress with the nearby Evergreen pack and meets Denton Arguson, Evergreen alpha, to ask for his help. Fate has a strange twist for both of them, though, and Mikael and Denton soon realize they're destined mates.

Denton resists the pull between them—he has his own pack and his own responsibilities. But Mikael isn't willing to give up. The Mother has promised Mikael his mate, told him he must fight for him, and that only together can they defeat the coming darkness. When Anton casts his sights on Denton's pack, attacks and sabotage follow, pulling Denton and Mikael together to defeat a common enemy. But Anton's threats sow seeds of destruction enough to break any bond, and the mates' determination to challenge the darkness may be their only saving grace.

www.dreamspinnerpress.com

DIRK GREYSON is very much an outside kind of man. He loves travel and seeing new things. Dirk worked in corporate America for way too long and now spends his days writing, gardening, and taking care of the home he shares with his partner of more than two decades. He has a master's degree and all the other accessories that go with a corporate job. But he is most proud of the stories he tells and the life he's built. Dirk lives in Pennsylvania in a century-old home and is blessed with an amazing circle of friends.

Facebook: www.facebook.com/dirkgreyson
E-mail: dirkgreyson@comcast.net

AN
ASSASSIN'S
HOLIDAY

DIRK
GREYSON

Brick Colton has been hired to kill Santa Claus—or at least the kindhearted accountant playing Santa for the kids in an orphanage. Brick grew up in an orphanage himself, but that isn't the only thing bothering him about the contract on Robin Marvington's life. The details don't add up, and it's looking more and more like someone has set Robin up. As Brick investigates, Robin brings some much-needed cheer into his life, the light in Robin's soul reaching something in Brick's dark one. But all of that will end if they can't find the person who wants Robin dead.

DIRK GREYSON

DAY AND KNIGHT

Day and Knight: Book One

As former NSA, Dayton (Day) Ingram has national security chops and now works as a technical analyst for Scorpion. He longs for fieldwork, and scuttling an attack gives him his chance. He's smart, multilingual, and a technological wizard. But his opportunity comes with a hitch—a partner, Knighton (Knight), who is a real mystery. Despite countless hours of research, Day can find nothing on the agent, including his first name!

Former Marine Knight crawled into a bottle after losing his family. After drying out, he's offered one last chance: along with Day, stop a terrorist threat from the Yucatan. To get there without drawing suspicion, Day and Knight board a gay cruise, where the deeply closeted Day and equally closeted Knight must pose as a couple. Tensions run high as Knight communicates very little and Day bristles at Knight's heavy-handed need for control.

But after drinking too much, Day and Knight wake up in bed. *Together.* As they near their destination, they must learn to trust and rely on each other to infiltrate the terrorist camp and neutralize the plot aimed at the US's technological infrastructure, if they hope to have a life after the mission. One that might include each other.

www.dreamspinnerpress.com

DIRK GREYSON
SUN AND SHADOW

Sequel to *Day and Knight*
Day and Knight: Book Two

Dayton "Day" Ingram is recovering from an injury suffered in Mexico—and from his failed relationship with fellow Scorpion agent, Knight. While researching an old government document, Day realizes he might be holding the key to finding an artistic masterpiece lost since WWII.

But the Russians are looking for it too, and have a team in place in Eastern Europe hunting it down. Day and Knight are brought back together when they are charged with getting to the painting first.

Knight wants to leave Mexico and everything that happened there behind, and return to the life he had—except it wasn't much of a life. When he's partnered up with Day, keeping his distance proves to be challenging. But Day is as stubborn as Knight and isn't willing to let him walk away.

Their assignment leads them through Germany and Austria with agents hot on their tail—agents willing to do whatever it takes to get to the masterpiece first. If Day and Knight can live long enough to find the painting, they might also discover something even more precious—each other.

www.dreamspinnerpress.com

www.ingramcontent.com/pod-product-compliance
Lightning Source LLC
Chambersburg PA
CBHW060058260626
47160CB00005B/1707